GYRE

PAUL BELASIK

Copyright © 2017 Paul Belasik.

All rights reserved. No part of this book may be reproduced, stored, or transmitted by any means—whether auditory, graphic, mechanical, or electronic—without written permission of the author, except in the case of brief excerpts used in critical articles and reviews. Unauthorized reproduction of any part of this work is illegal and is punishable by law.

ISBN: 978-1-4834-7085-6 (sc)
ISBN: 978-1-4834-7084-9 (hc)
ISBN: 978-1-4834-7086-3 (e)

Library of Congress Control Number: 2017908804

Because of the dynamic nature of the Internet, any web addresses or links contained in this book may have changed since publication and may no longer be valid. The views expressed in this work are solely those of the author and do not necessarily reflect the views of the publisher, and the publisher hereby disclaims any responsibility for them.

Any people depicted in stock imagery provided by Thinkstock are models, and such images are being used for illustrative purposes only.
Certain stock imagery © Thinkstock.

Lulu Publishing Services rev. date: 8/31/2017

For Tom Maechtle

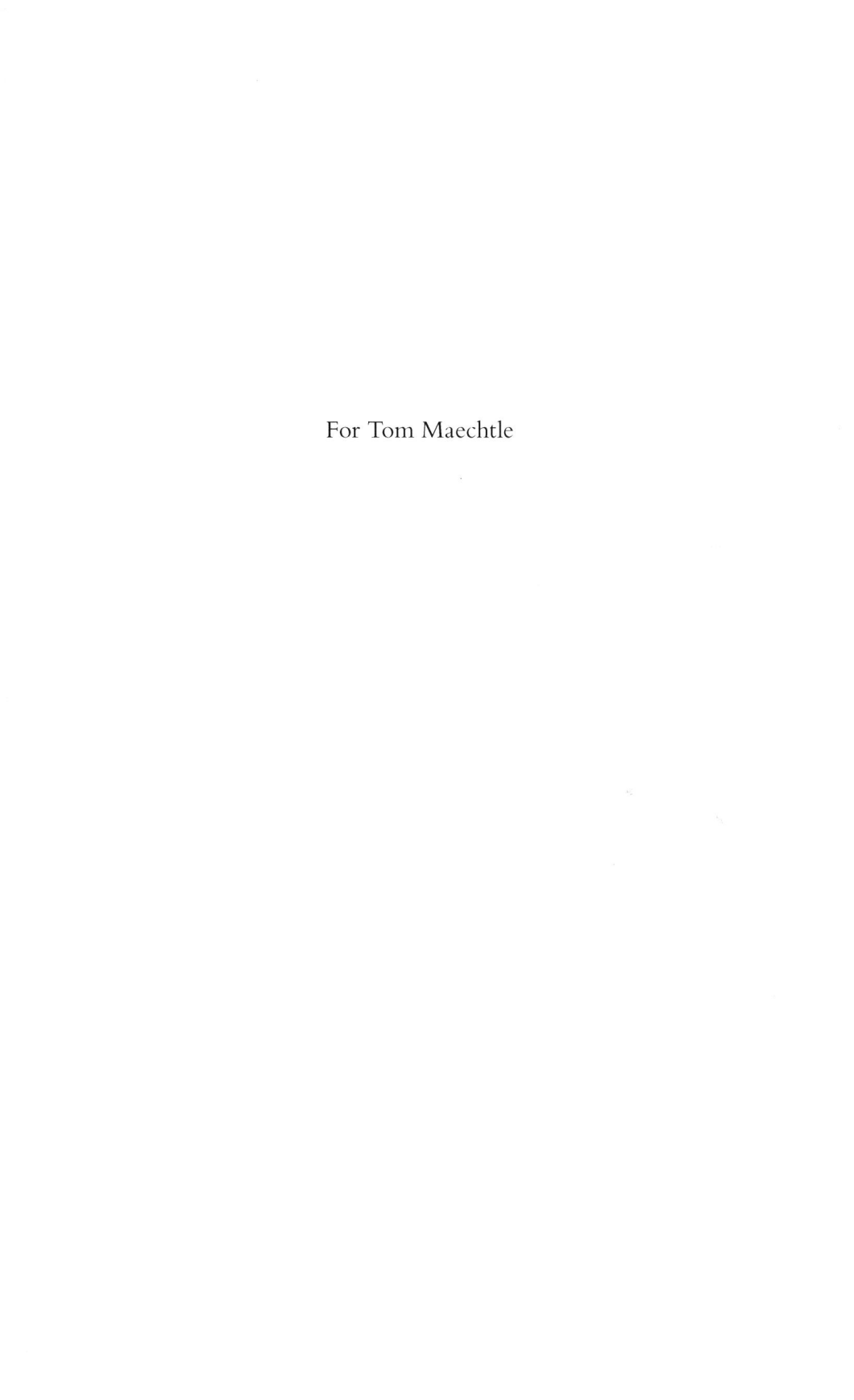

Prologue

They were descendants of the B'Tai, who lived here before countries had names, when people were just a few fleas on the majestic hide of the earth. They were the oldest horse people the world has ever known. They were the people who found falconry, the knowledge of freedom and death. The little boy and his father belonged to a nomadic group of Buddhist Mongols. They had collected a few horses and were making their way back out of the sharp foothills that spilled from the mountains behind them. The mountains went up beyond all trees, beyond breathable air into spires that many days were obscured by clouds of their own, knife-edges disguised by whipping plumes, snow tails and flags. The mountains went on behind them as far as the eye could see in either direction. It would take weeks to return to the camp on the vast plain where the boy's mother and sisters spent the summer on the endless flat grasslands, tan now at the end of summer. Rare outcrops of rock percolated out of the flatness, the only hint that something below could rise or had risen just a little farther away with unimaginable power and violence and continued to agitate the sky. The plain was where they mostly lived, where his father and his uncle hunted with eagles.

On the plain, there was not a tree in sight. Even after days of riding, it was all sky; no place for an errant eagle to roost or get lost. If any game appeared, the chase could be on. The eagle and the horse had extended the killing arms and legs of the man. They helped him to survive in this vastness. It was there in his first summers that the little boy learned to imitate the call of his father's eagle. It still brought a smile to his father's face every time the boy made the unmistakable sound.

For now, they were a long way from the plain. They were picking their way down the bony, fanning ridges and ravines that fell toward the steppe. These were places where wild horses could escape the summer insects and each other, where young stallions that had been shunned from their mothers' herds had a chance to find their own mares.

The father knew it was time to head back. From easy riding to treacherous, leg-breaking descents, the horses stumbled their way through rocky, barren slopes and sliding scree, grazed their way through alpine meadows. In this land of extremes, the weather had the same character. Tiny specks on the enormous landscape, father and son and horses were descending through a section of woods when a wind came up and in a matter of minutes brought a cloud of snow that they might have seen coming if they were out in the open. A blizzarding wall of wet snow and cold air came at them out of the mountains and the little flea stars were instantly plunged into a blinding, howling nebula. The father was ahead, leading on an older stallion. The boy was at the back on a younger stallion. When the father turned he could not even see the horses behind him, much less the little boy. The icy snow stung his face and eyes, but he pushed his horse back toward the place where he had last seen his son. The little boy ducked his face into the long hair on his horse's neck. It filtered the suffocating sharpness so that he could breathe. The young stallion could feel the older stallion coming toward them. He knew it was a chance to take at least the one mare next to him and steal her for himself. So he carefully, slowly and steadily moved her over the edge of the ridge they were coming down. The boy raised his head, his eyes shut against the storm, and called for his father. The father called for the boy. There was only a slight chance that between the sustained wind that used every tree and rock and needle to amplify itself into a cacophonous anti-music and the immediate muffling of the heavy snow that they could have ever heard each other, and that chance was gone when the young stallion broke over the ridge and cut off all connecting sound. By the time the father got to the area where his son had been, there was only fresh snow. A clean, deepening blanket had already covered up any tracks. The old stallion knew where the young stallion had gone and he would have followed him to get his mare back, but the father turned him away from the ridge in the opposite direction. Throughout the night, the boy screamed for his father. He used the eagle call, everything he could think of. His face was frozen from his tears. He held the horse tight for any warmth and comfort, even as the horse steadily moved him further and further away from his father. The next day, the storm still churned. The boy was wet and freezing, his voice was a rasping whisper. He knew he had to try to eat. A thousand times, when he was very little, his mother had held him next to her chest as she milked the mares. He got down off his horse. He was shivering, staggering through the snow as he approached the mare. She had been bred for the first time that year, so she had no foal. She had no milk. The boy struggled back toward the young stallion, but the stallion walked away from him.

By the time the wolves got to the boy there was little life left, the body was shutting down. He had stopped shivering and his consciousness was restless. It was getting ready to move. The first wolf slunk down with its ears back and crawled toward the boy. Snarling in a snapping motion, it grabbed the sleeve of the boy's coat and tugged. The boy fell stiffly toward the wolf in a lurch. The wolf yelped and jumped hysterically to the side. From a little further away, the largest wolf of the pack walked calmly forward. When it was close to the boy, it rocked back onto its hindquarters and leaped up in an arc, transferring all the power from its hind legs through the great arch of his back into his powerful shoulders, thick neck and massive head, the motion gaining power like a giant wave. His jaws crushed into the base of the boy's skull and his spine, the massive vice mercifully finishing the boy's pain. They ate even the boy's clothing. There was no trace left. No one ever found anything.

CHAPTER ONE

Cross Keys, Montana
McPherson Psychiatric Clinic

Robert McPherson looked out the window of his office again. The weather was perfect for hawking. He made a few more business calls, then phoned his old friend Sam Lindley, a falconer's falconer.

"Sam, it's Bob. Hey, I'm in the office. I was supposed to have the day off but Marilyn's son is sick, so she stayed home and I'm catching up on a few things. I've got a few more calls to make, but what I was hoping to do is get Griffin out for some training. He's been doing well, but he needs experience. I really have to get him working - I feel badly always tagging along with you, using your dogs."

"You know that's not a problem."

"Well, I appreciate that. I was wondering if you were going to fly any of your birds this afternoon. I'm afraid that if I take my bird out to try to train Griff and he makes a mistake that I'm going to have a lost dog and a lost hawk. If I could concentrate - ".

Sam cut him off. "I'm actually halfway to the Robinson's ranch. I can fly my two young falcons first. If you can get out here by around four, I'll fly Miro last and you can work your dog."

Bob sighed with relief. "I was hoping you would come up with something like that."

Miro was a veteran. Sam had hunted him for almost twelve years. If things went wrong, Bob knew Sam could call Miro back to his fist practically anytime. It would take pressure off Robert and Griff. If he made a mistake, he wouldn't upset a more sensitive falcon into flying off.

Sam told Bob to meet him at the third watering pond; if either had a change they would call the other.

Bob and Sam had been friends for a long time. They met in college through falconry, but Bob's medical studies and then his psychiatric practice took the forefront and although he tried through the years to hunt some kind of hawk, it was a secondary passion.

Sam Lindley, on the other hand, folded his childhood passion for falcons into his career as a biologist. Sam, like all falconers, knew that this primitive art form, with its rituals of elegant dying, was a string back to the past and understanding himself. He felt like an adopted child. He wasn't ungrateful to those who raised him and cared for him, but he had haunting feelings of interrupted connections, deep in his DNA. He was sure if he followed the string of falconry, it could tell him who he really was, what he really was. If he wanted to pursue this string theory, he needed falcons. In 1960, after 3,500 years of falconry, this was not a given.

In their first years in college, the world was taking notice of a precipitous drop in the population of peregrine falcons, especially across the North American continent. By pure luck, a center of research began at the university they were attending, so they volunteered and worked for free at the hawk barns.

Pesticides were highly suspect, but to make a case data had to be collected and damaged eggs had to be gathered and analyzed. Falcons don't nest in trees. They thrive in spectacularly inaccessible country where they lay their eggs on scrapes of rock, specifically selected barren depressions of stone, high on the face of a cliff. Where Robert could only volunteer some time for menial work at the hawk lab, Sam fell from the beginning into the adventure of a lifetime. He spent summers in the arctic creating a census of nest sites and collecting damaged eggs. He climbed mountains, rappelled off cliff edges, kayaked up ice-cold rivers, often camped out in the tundra alone. It was the beginning of his habit of spending too many days and too much of his time thinking more like a falcon than a human being.

DDT turned out to be the culprit, weakening eggshell walls so they couldn't hatch, but DDT was a big tool in the arsenal of pesticides that were essential for commercial agriculture. The big business of agriculture, with its powerful hands in government, was not about to relinquish the incredible effectiveness of DDT. Some beautiful politics were required to nurse the beautiful science of falcon recovery. An odd collection of scientists and senators, soldiers and hippies, antisocial falconers and zealous environmentalists, eccentric bird watchers and conscienceless businessmen all worked together. Even as they succeeded in eliminating DDT, a whole population of new birds had be artificially bred and reestablished in the wild. Once again Sam was involved. He helped by establishing hacking sites, often at the hauntingly empty sites that falcons had previously returned to, year after year. The new hacking sites had to be private places where young laboratory-bred birds could be set out and fed with hidden human contact until they could fly off, as they might from natural nurseries. It would have been an impossible drama, except that the central character in this passion play was one of the most glamorous animals nature has ever produced. Falcons had the power to push people past their biographies and biases.

If an attack of a falcon was seen in slow motion, it would seem that the bird would surely break apart. At ridiculous altitudes, the falcon stops pumping its wings and folds itself for a stoop that can exceed two hundred miles an hour. Its plummeting body quivers, seemingly near the limits of its design like an experimental aircraft. If the falcon's strike on the prey does not result in the prey's instant death, the falcon may pursue, huge talons swinging one way, body gyrating another, one wing braking and bending at a grotesque angle, the other wing pointed down, stretched like a Chinese fan. Quickly, the falcon's body unifies again and smoothly accelerates toward the prey, guided by the locking in of its giant black eyes on their target. Falcons don't lie at the bottom of the ocean pretending to be something else, hoping to trap some careless, unsuspecting prey. Falcons don't stealthily prowl in the brush or wait for the cover of darkness. Falcons levitate, often from long periods of sleep. They send themselves up into a wide-open sky. Everything is warned. They are that confident.

If the flight of hunting is always about death, a solemn martial affair, the flights of courtship are something else entirely, a mobile creation. Every movement learned in and for aggression can be embellished to impress and new ones can be improved upon. After barrel rolls, loop-de-loops, and flying completely upside down, the two acrobatic birds might tangle and hold each other, dropping a thousand feet at terminal velocity, releasing each other at the last possible moment and slicing back up into the sky with unimaginable G-forces. It is arguably the finest of flying because it is flight for flight's sake alone. How well can you fly, not how well you can kill.

No white person had seen more of this aerial high art than Sam in the years he spent in the arctic. There was no question that there were hunting flights that were staggeringly impressive. If the prey was a good flier itself and was convinced that its life was at stake, there would be maximum efforts and mesmerizing results, but none would contain the sensual, symphonic passes woven into the virtuosic solos of courtship flights. Courtship flights might look like hunting, but are something else entirely, the real goal only to be beautiful, alluring, arresting. The falcons taught Sam about all kinds of flight and how to observe, how to hold outcome in suspension. Even with the strongest falcons and the most perfect flights, the outcome was never certain. He learned that no matter how well trained he was, he could not be sure what was going to happen. Where many people found this unsettling, Sam found freedom and solace, realizing that no one could plan out their life, or his. His study of biology was informing an artist's philosophy: work hard, don't trap yourself with expectations, and leave room for chance. The metaphor of falconry never escaped him. He became addicted to it and used it throughout his life, like other people used weekly church services to revitalize themselves, to humble themselves, to strengthen themselves, to handle the mundane. When later in his life he said things like, "I don't really know what will happen next," most people thought it was just laissez-fair, but what he meant was, "I have learned to let life happen to me." Few people realized the depth of the underlying wisdom that had been infused in a young mind trained directly by nature itself.

Sam saw the falcons, but he also heard them and felt them. Waiting on cliff edges until he thought at least one of a pair were off hunting, he would rappel down a cliff face to a nest scrape to check or collect eggs. Invariably, the escorting fighter jets would return. At four times the weight of a baseball and at speeds far exceeding the limits of a professional baseball pitcher, the agitated projectiles pushed, intimidated and threatened as they shot past him. They sliced his clothes and his skin. It was then, hanging from a rope with his face pressed to the rock wall, that he learned about their sounds. Not just the screeches and kaks, not just the sounds of voice; it also was the sensation of sound when a two-pound object flying through the friction of air at near terminal velocity passed inches from his head. It was impossible not to reflexively spasm his body toward some fetal crouch when the sounds became louder and more frequent, with double-teaming rapier attacks. He used to wonder why the day after those climbs his neck hurt more than any other part of his body. He learned how sound can hurt.

It was in the arctic that he saw his first wild gyr falcons, the largest and strongest of all the falconidae, the circumpolar hunters that are sometimes pure white and are one of the most stunning animals on earth. Up there, while working on migrations, Sam linked up with people in the defense department, which gave him access to some of the most sophisticated satellite tracking devices. Working with the military, he became an expert in telemetry. In the beginning, falconers and soldiers each had their own agenda, but Sam and other falconers his age thought the trade-off was acceptable. They were old enough to remember losing hawks before the feather-light tracking devices. They knew the sinking feeling of watching something so important disappear, then traipsing around after dark in hope of finding the bird roosting for the night or getting up in the dark the next day, returning to the place of the last sighting, looking, calling, straining their ears to hear the faintest tinkle of the bells attached to the falcon's legs. Bells they saved their money for to buy from Pakistan because they thought they were the bells with the purest tones that would carry the sound the farthest. The bells had been beautiful, but telemetry was better.

Sam was involved in it all. His resume read like a novel and because of his sincere personality and reputation for tireless work he could contact nearly any expert on raptors in the world and they would answer his call. From an early age, Sam was hooked on powerful things. It became difficult for him to return from another adventure and adjust to the rhythms of a more normal life. When he was in Russia or Greenland, he needed guides and interpreters, and he found that he needed a similar sort of thing back in the States. When he met Jane Petersen, a writer from Wyoming, it was perfect. She loved him, and she loved to talk about him. She became his interpreter. She reminded him about outgoing thank-you's, phone calls, social events, and explained incoming emotions. She was clairvoyant at managing the space around him. When regular life would begin to get him stressed, she would take over some little job and give him some relief. She would send him to the hardware store, casually opening a window for him to breathe. She gave him plenty of freedom and almost never forced him to explain himself. Even inside the house, he never felt cornered. He knew she was becoming indispensable and that people assumed what she said was what he thought. He just didn't care enough about what most people thought to clear things up, which of course led to more people misunderstanding him. That didn't matter. He was comfortable with a smaller and smaller constellation of friends.

They had three daughters who grew up understanding that the cute little ducks, quail, pigeons and chickens that they helped raise and name were for the most part sacrifices for the feeding and training of falcons. Sam loved the girls; he was always patient with them, but never coddling. They seemed to vacillate from pride in their father, when someone important cited him, to feeling sick of his "obsession with killing," which they brought up to him whenever they thought they needed to. They all could document their disgust with stories of coming out of the house looking for him to help with homework and calmly discussing a math problem while in his bloody hands he would be holding some freshly killed little quail because it was feeding time for the falcons. Growing up in a world of unusually uncensored passion, and understanding the violence and beauty of nature, none of them was anyone's fool. They learned directly the subtleties of predation. They knew its disguises. They were well schooled in how to separate language from actions. Early on, they were little philosophers with a sense of the street. As they grew older, their attitude seemed to become almost protective of Sam, whom they saw as more of an absent-minded professor than a wild man hanging off cliff faces.

In the first attempts to breed a base of falcons to return to the wild, researchers found that wild caught birds would almost never breed in captivity. Once wild, the stress of captivity was consuming and it affected everything about the birds. They could not be brought in from the big spaces and stay healthy. What saved the species was that it was possible in a laboratory to artificially breed birds and raise their chicks, then turn the chicks loose to become wild. It just couldn't be turned around. That is what happened to Sam Lindley. Over time, his personal chemistry changed. He became more and more feral. Jane's role as a social buffer only contributed to his reclusiveness.

Bob McPherson noticed Sam could not come back east anymore, not without a lot of stress. It was not eccentricity or affectation. Bob was certain if he ran a blood test on Sam during trips back east, he would see cortisol levels through the roof. He was only comfortable in the wide-open west. It was no mystery why Sam liked to fly gyr falcons. They needed the most space. If Sam was exploring bigger and bigger space outside himself, Robert had been going the opposite way – more and more into the internal space.

Robert McPherson was an only child. His father was a musician's musician, totally unknown except to serious guitar players. He was born in Scotland and moved to the States when he married Bob's mother, an American whom he met in Edinburgh when she was an exchange student. From his father, Bob learned to play the guitar and to appreciate music. He inherited his father's voice and good looks, the combination of that made him interesting to women throughout his life. He also inherited the Scottish love of a good time. It took him a while to learn to balance these things. If he received a heavier dose of genetic predisposition that directed his life, it was from his mother. His mother was a nurse who had an overpowering affinity with children. She had never met a baby she didn't think was arrestingly beautiful. She would look at each one and find some feature that was special and rare, this one's jaw, this one's hands, the way this one seemed to think. Every new mother who let Anna McPherson look at or hold her child (and she always held their child; she simply weaned them out of the mother's hands) would be changed. One could physically see the new trepidation, the delicacy in the mother's hands and arms as Anna gave the child back. She had convinced them in a very short time that this child was a very special child, part of some divinity, and the mother had a societal responsibility which accompanied giving birth to this mystery. Bob realized, growing up with her, that the reason she was so convincing was because she believed it. In her eyes, there could never be such a thing as an ugly child. It was a philosophical statement that emanated from her physical chemistry. She was hardwired with an overdeveloped sense of responsibility to a child's vulnerability and potential. On top of that, she had a sanctified Arthurian duty to protect these mysteries. Robert McPherson inherited his mother's ability to be spellbound by children and their innocence. He knew it could be a weakness when he found himself becoming overprotective. He would remind himself that his mother insisted it was her job to keep them healthy. They needed to be strong so they could rebound when they eventually got hurt, falling out of love, falling off a horse, falling off a mountain. She would be there to patch them up. She didn't talk that much about keeping them safe, she never wanted to see children wrapped up and insulated from life. She thought it was pernicious to look at all that possibility and then start blocking it from developing in a world that was not always nice. This all probably had something to do with why Robert didn't have children. His line of work could be so consuming and heart-breaking that he felt perhaps he didn't have enough left for children of his own. But maybe he had never found the right woman, and he knew he couldn't do it alone.

Robert McPherson was not a particularly lucky person, but if he had one rabbit's foot, it was a big one, and that was his knack for finding the best teachers. Maybe it started back with his father and music where he saw good teaching and good learning. He could see the earnestness of the people who sought his father out and appeared at their house to learn. Throughout his life and career when he wanted to learn something, a first class mentor would appear. In Chicago, it was Archie Hathaway, the head of Psychiatry at the hospital where Robert worked. Hathaway was a gifted psychotherapist, self-critical, a great counter puncher to his own flexible mind. He was also at the forefront of psychopharmacology when it was getting started. It seemed like he constantly struggled with the limits of both. He was a warm person, sophisticated, but without airs. One year, Robert remembered, for a kind of sabbatical, Archie was going to spend a year in Italy and touring Europe. He and his wife came back after a month and all he would say is "Europe is too old!" And yet Archie was fascinated by Buddhism and practiced silently. He and Robert became friends; even after Robert left Chicago, he would see Archie at least once a year. In the later years, they didn't talk about medicine anymore. They would have coffee and Archie's wife would usually find some excuse to leave so they could have some time to themselves. It was only in his home that he could see Archie's Buddhist leanings. In the last couple of weeks, before he died, two young monks came to his house every day and worked on an intricate sand painting, scratching away with small metal funnels filled with different colors of sand. Meticulously, they created a beautiful mandala. On the day he died, they carefully walked it down to the lake in front of his house and brushed the masterpiece into the water.

Sam and Bob did not see much of each other after college, but their lives came back together about seven years ago when Robert's wife, Maggie Serano, was offered a chair in the psychiatric department at the University of Montana. Maggie wasn't sure she could live forever out west, but the position was enticing. She could hear her father Augustine reminding people to never be in a position where they are not looking for a job. It was a step up for her career. Robert's career had become a totally private practice so he had a certain flexibility to move. With Jane and Margaret's connection with horses, and Sam and Bob's long history with falconry, with Bob and Margaret having no children and vicariously enjoying Sam and Jane's three, it was perfect. In a part of the country that did not necessarily encourage social interaction, the only problem seemed to be that in between their jobs and their own sets of friends, they didn't have enough time to spend together.

Bob was in his office trying to finish some work so he could get out to see Sam and hunt the young dog. School was now in full swing and he knew business was about to pick up; the usual problems with children, and the usual problems between professional teachers and unprofessional parents of children with problems that they mostly created. Although there were extremes of wealth in the state, almost all the people, rich or poor, spent a lot of time outdoors. There was a pervasive mountain climber mystique in the culture. People romanticized risk and carried self-determination to a form of idolatry. It could be hard on children growing up here. There weren't many kids to socialize with, so peer pressure was distilled and could be intense. In some counties, drugs were epidemic. Youthful mistakes in judgment could be expensive in this wild country.

The office phone rang. Bob was going to let it go to the automated message, but he picked it up.

"McPherson Clinic."

"Hello, my name is Patricia Nelson. We've recently moved to the area. My son is enrolled in Grover, he's been in therapy for a number of years." The woman's voice was soft but her introduction was memorized, she had done this before. "Dr. McPherson and his wife were highly recommended."

Bob interrupted her gently. "Mrs. Nelson, I'm Robert McPherson. I have to tell you that my wife teaches at the University, but she is not part of the practice, if that makes a difference."

"Well, no, Doctor. What I was calling about was to see if you were accepting new patients."

"Yes, I am. I apologize for my phone etiquette. My secretary's son is sick, so she's out of the office today. She's better at this than I am. Normally, I like to meet the parents and the child first, then review any medical records. My secretary's name is Marilyn Banks. She will be in tomorrow. I'll make a note for her to call you back and we can set up an appointment. How does that sound?"

"That would be perfect."

"Mrs. Nelson, what is your son's name?"

"Sean."

"That was my father's name. Ok, please give me your number and Marilyn will be in touch with you tomorrow."

"Thank you, Doctor."

Robert took down the information and thanked her for calling.

When she hung up the phone, Patricia Nelson thought it was a little unusual that Robert McPherson didn't ask anything about the problem, only her son's name. Still, somehow she had a nice feeling about him. He answered his own phone, he asked her son's name. Maybe that's how it's done out here, she thought.

Robert hung up the phone, wrote a note for his secretary, and then called his wife. He knew she would be at a meeting or teaching. The phone transferred him to messages.

"Maggie, hi, I just talked to Sam. I'm going to work Griff with his birds this afternoon, so I don't think I'll be home before dark. You are probably going to ride, so what if I call you when I'm on my way home and we can work something out for dinner. Let me know if that's not ok. Bye," he said gently. Click.

He glanced around the office and checked his schedule for tomorrow. Satisfied, he locked the door and left for home.

Within an hour, Robert had fed his peregrine falcon and secured her for the evening. He picked up Griffin, who already knew they were going hunting when Robert pulled in the driveway. Griffin was a beautiful dog. A little on the large size for a setter, he was powerful. His long base coat of white was splattered with patches of black and tipped with small spots of deep rich brown. In some places, he looked like an exquisitely crafted modern painting and in other places he looked like a painter's old drop cloth. He had a black mask that made him look like a bandit and a long white tail that swung one way or another when he hunted to counterbalance the sharp zigzagging of his body as he methodically worked huge sections of ground searching for birds. If he found birds, everything would stop, his white tail flagged straight up, motionless except for the air currents waving the long, soft strands. When Bob was really close to him, he could faintly detect all the contained excitement creating a tremolo throughout Griff's body, the tips of his hair minutely vibrating. He had to be taught to ignore the antelope or deer or rabbits that might tear off in front of him. All the instinct to chase had to be funneled into one job. These dogs were specialists even among bird hunting dogs because they worked for specialists. They weren't working a single area limited to a few yards in front of a slow moving human being with a shotgun. They were working under a trolling falcon that could be forty miles away in a half an hour. Griffin had the searching down, he could cover vast amounts of ground and he was thorough, but he needed more experience in the cat and mouse game when he did find a covey of birds. The grouse doesn't want to blast off in an intense escape if it doesn't have to; it costs too much energy. It will wait and measure the threat. A good hunting dog will search by scent and when it gets close, slam on the brakes and very gently get closer to see if there are any birds or it's just left over scent from where they had been. It is all about space and time. Give the birds enough space and they may wait, crouch, and freeze, hoping the threat will pass by. This space gives the hunter time. Time to make sure the falcon is in a good position. All the while the dog must be in motionless control, waiting for a signal from the human. If the birds try to creep away, he may close in on them to freeze them. If he flushes them too early, and the falcon knows it doesn't have a chance to catch them, the falcon may lose interest or feel it can do better on its own and take off, never to be seen again. There isn't a lot of room for mistakes. That is why Robert wanted to hunt Griffin under Sam's oldest bird, a gyrfalcon named Miro. Sam and Miro had hunted for many years and Robert knew if Griffin made a mistake, Sam could call Miro back by swinging a lure with a bit of food on it or calling him straight back to his fist. Miro would not get rattled if a young dog did something odd. Miro seemed comfortable with his arrangement with Sam. He never had to worry if prey was short or storms prevented him from hunting. Sam took care of him; he had excellent food ready every day. So for the better part of a decade, Miro hunted for Sam for a few months in return for his secure care for rest of the year. If he wasn't comfortable with the arrangement on any hunting day he could have flown off, but he never did. They seemed to like each other.

Once Bob turned off the highway at Route 15, he entered a small dirt road that quickly turned into nothing more than a two-track path. When he bumped off the highway, Griffin picked up his head, waking from his nap. Although he had an expensive and elaborate kennel in the back of the pickup truck, when Robert was alone he let Griffin ride in the back seat. Even though he was a hunting dog, he was also a family pet.

The beginning of the dirt road traced the boundary of two large ranches before it turned right toward the heart of the Robinson's ranch. He was still thirty minutes from the pond where he had agreed to meet Sam. Both ranches were thousands of acres. The people who owned the ranches did not live here. They came for vacations in the summer or to hunt in the fall or ski in the winter. They bought the ranches for different reasons, but almost never to come here to live full time. No matter what the people looked like, how they dressed in cowboy hats or boots, immediately or distantly they were all easterners. No matter how strong their motivation was to get away from something in the past, they seemed to drag along chunks of the culture they were trying to escape. It might be the subtle social snobbery in some family's penchant for antique furniture for houses half the antiques' age or it might be a more virulent form of the culture of cultivation, the culture of tearing up the land.

Someone had to manage these ranches. Ironically, some of the best managers were children of the absentee owners. They might be the odd child in the family who never did well in the elite schools. They didn't fit in. They came out on vacation when they were young and fell in love with the freedom of the country. Eventually, they never went back, they made themselves into hunting guides, fly fishing experts, artists, heads of non-profits. Although they often left a slightly unpleasant scent of noblesse oblige in their wake, they seemed better for the land and for the animals, including the people. The worst managers were people who saw all that space as fallow and thought the lazy land needed a job, it needed to make some money. Modern cattle ranching was probably the most inefficient way to feed people ever dreamed up. But on the right side of politics, with the right tax advantages and lease agreements, with a little creativity in arithmetic, it could be called a viable business. Those with bigger ideas, leaned toward mining or oil and gas exploration instead of ranching.

Where Robert was, on the two-track path following the rickety wire fence lines that marked the division of these two great holdings, there was a clear example of the different ways of thinking. Off to the right of the bouncing truck was sagebrush following the gentle contours of the flattish land all the way to the base of the distant mountains that were the beginnings of the long spine of the Rockies. It was arid country, high desert. The tough, knee-to-thigh-high bushes of sage had deep roots to search for the scarce water and this helped to hold the dry soil from blowing away. In the winter, the bushes formed miles and miles of snow fence, trapping windblown snow, capturing it to be melted slowly into precious water by the warming spring sun. The sage fed the grouse and the antelope and they in turn fed the hawks, eagles and lions. Robert's truck spooked a herd of Pronghorn antelope. They burst clattering down a shallow depression and then up a low canyon wall, leaving a trail of dust in the air behind them. They crested the rim and ran along the skyline in silhouette for a half mile until they turned farther west out of sight. To understand the importance of sage, it is not necessary to study the ecology. Just get out and walk through it for a few minutes. Its heavy scent immediately informs you of its significance: thick, calming, medicinal. It is easy to see why it was so important to the native people. Where Robert and Sam were hunting was so untouched by cultivation that there were still teepee rings. Circles of stone on high spots or near water marked favorite camping sites of the Indians who used the stones to hold down the edges of the skin tarp coverings of their nomadic dwellings. Every time they drove out here, Robert marveled at the distance these people covered on foot or horseback. On the other hand, off to the left of his truck, was endless, waving grassland. It looked pretty, the way the reddish yellow wheat fields in Nebraska can dip and dance behind an invisible current of wind. Here, thousands of acres of sage were systematically killed off with herbicides from airplanes so grasses could be replanted for grazing cattle. Species of grass that weren't even native, grasses that were ecologically useless. They couldn't hold snow and sucked up the surface water so fast it made the dry country even drier. There was nothing for the sage grouse to eat and not much more for anything else that naturally lived out there. In the summer, it was nothing more than a ten-mile match head, tempting the lightning.

Robert knew that one of the reasons Sam began hunting at the ponds was that the sage grouse population was declining. It didn't matter that the cause was diminishing habitat. If they were declared endangered, the privilege of hunting them would be lost. So just in case, Sam began to fly a little at ducks, even though they would never test the gyrs like the strong acrobatic flights of the sage grouse. Falconers had a firsthand reading of ecologic trends. They noticed the problems early, but they were careful with politics and tried to be polite. They needed a lot of room to fly their birds. They had to know all the owners and ranch managers. Regardless of their politics, they needed their permission to hunt or in some cases just to cross their land, open a gate, or use a road to retrieve a lost bird. They knew everything that was going on, but they were very careful with their comments.

Finally, Robert drove over a small crest and could see Sam's truck parked near the pond. The water levels were down now, in the dry fall. He slowed, in case Sam had a bird out and gently rolled in near Sam's truck. He got out and quietly closed the door. From now on they kept their voices down. Robert had a theory that falconers were sarcastic because they couldn't tell sidesplitting, howling laughter jokes when they were around the birds. They developed a softer but wittier sense of humor, as dry as some of the country they were in. Robert could crack Sam up, though. It was easier in the old days when they would get into the tequila, but he could still do it. It was so satisfying to break through that stoic reserve. Robert knew when he had Sam because he would start squinting, his eyes smiling already. Then he would wince as if he were in considerable pain, trying to hold it in and keep things under control. But by then it was too late, the façade would have melted and the purest, childlike, joyful laughter would roll out of his completely softened face. Robert loved to make his friend laugh that hard, and with anyone else except Robert, Sam would be embarrassed by it. They seemed so different. One was always mining emotions to the surface, and the other trying to bury them deep in the salt. Yet with falconry, they got the same relief from getting outside of whom they had become (not all of which they liked) into a place that was beautiful and unpredictable, where they had to pay attention and forget about everything else for a while.

"Hey, taking a nap?" Robert saw him still in the truck.

Sam got out. "How are you?"

"Fine. I'm not late, am I?"

"No, no, you're fine. I flew the other two and it went well, so I thought I would leave it at that."

"Sam, I really appreciate this. I think Griff will be fine, but this will really help."

Sam began to prepare Miro and Robert let Griff out of the truck to loosen up. Part of the scene, the sights and sounds were ancient. The falcons standing on perches, wearing intricately hand sewn burnished leather hoods to keep them quiet in travel, each with a small decorative plume on top. The bells on their legs chimed lightly as they changed their stance or stretched out a wing or leg. The dog rustling through the dry brush ranged out, little by little, farther away from the truck. It had been done this way for thousands of years. There was tradition and method in preparing for something to be killed. Everyone was serious. The mind of the falconer gets trained by experience. It registers adrenaline, panic. It registers calmness and integrity. Whether the falconer realizes it or not, he begins to learn how to die, and in turn, this tells him how to live. As Sam went to get Miro, he first reached in to fit Miro's leg with a lightweight telemetry bracelet, as tricky to connect as a woman's thin necklace. Sam had to be careful to keep his bare hands out of the way of the talons. If the bird got impatient and stamped, it would be painful if his hand was in the way of one of the knife-like talons, even if the bird didn't squeeze. Then he checked the signals. In the truck, he had a small number of receivers; each falcon had its own signal. If a bird went out of sight, Sam could turn on the receiver and scan the sky with a small hand held antennae and listen for a locating beep. The closer the bird, the stronger or faster the beep. It was one of the few modern electronic beeps that was not annoying. Robert fitted a similar device to Griff's collar. That way the dog could be located; if it was deep in some cover and on a serious point, an impatient hunter wouldn't call him back because he couldn't see him.

Their plan was to work the bowl where Sam had seen some grouse earlier. Robert kept Griff in range, but he let him start to work a little. He was off back and forth in curving lines, following his nose. The sun glinted off his white coat like the phosphorescent albedo of snow, in and out of sight, as he wove through the mazes of the brush. Sam had Miro out on his gloved fist. Even though the glove protected his flesh from the sharpness of Miro's talons, he could still feel the strong surges of pressure as the bird rebalanced itself. Once the bird was on Sam's fist, that hand was occupied, leaving

Sam only one hand and his teeth to adjust the hood, his face inches from Miro's sharp and powerful beak. Sam deftly slipped the hood off Miro and revealed the secret weapon of falcons, those massive dark eyes. Up close, unhooding a falcon is like opening a box and revealing some huge jewel; the eyes shocking on a primal level. Miro shook his feathers and majestically looked left and right, as if in one scan he could collect all the information he would need. It is probably impossible for a human to understand the acuity and scope of these lenses, capable of detecting the movement of a mouse at a mile. The advantage is incalculable. His feathers fell flat against his body, a body that by weight is one of the strongest on the earth. It is still unknown how falcons can generate enough power to lift and carry off prey that weigh substantially more than they do. Since their muscles are hidden beneath the slick, exquisitely edged feathers, you cannot marvel at the body of a bird like you can marvel at the body of a horse. Sam knew better than to take it for granted. Sam held his arm out; a good falconer just waits and lets the bird get ready. Falcons can rest for long periods of time like a cat, and when they want to move, they define grace and power. When Miro felt right, he pushed off Sam's firm arm, which sunk down from the force of the bird's wings. The bird dropped a couple feet and in a matter of seconds the powerful strokes of his wings had him way above their heads, climbing in wider and wider rings.

Now, everything was at the service of the hawk, so the hawk can in turn serve the man and the dog. Griffin began working the sagebrush out into the long depression of land. The flag of his tail slashed around the muted, smoky green brush. The two men started following the dog and Miro, almost out of sight at times, followed all of them in long loops like a jet in a holding pattern.

Sam was so knowledgeable about how falcons feel that he was one of only a few people in the world who successfully bred falcons without artificial insemination or incubation, using no laboratory, seemingly no science at all, except the art of making wild birds so comfortable that they would breed and raise their young as if they were all alone in Greenland. I just throw them together, he would say. This coming from a man who knew and tried every new technique, no matter how suspect, until he knew for himself whether or not it had merit. When Jane and his daughters found him spending extra hours in the shop or waiting silently each day for some package to be delivered, they would all look at each other, wondering what the mad professor was up to now. Sam was one of the first falconers to try to use weather balloons to train the falcons for higher climbs by luring them up high with the balloons in order to get more spectacular stoops. The balloons were not cheap, and his girls got a lots of mileage out of watching him struggle to get the gas filled air bags into a trailer. They had even more fun when he sheepishly came home, having lost another one in space.

Miro was a veteran now and he wasn't going to waste time climbing higher than he had to, just for show. Even though he was older and slower, he was still deadly with his cunning. It wasn't long before Griffin slowed and then stiffened his tail straight up, long white hairs shimmering from his quaking nerves. Robert got close enough to make sure he could remind him to wait if he needed to. Sam looked for Miro. He had just turned past them, so they would have to wait until he came around the great arc and was heading toward them again to see everything. Griffin waited. The men stood still. The falcon curved back and was gaining ground toward them. When he was almost above them, Sam gave a signal for Robert to send in Griff and in perfect harmony the dog flushed the covey of grouse. Six grouse exploded in all directions like Fourth of July fireworks. Sam hooted loudly to alert Miro in case he was daydreaming, but he was way ahead of it all. He had seen everything and already was pumping upward. When he felt he had enough height, he folded his wings and dove down and down, gaining incredible speed. From far away it looked utterly smooth, but the falcon rattled in the forces like a bobsled on ice. He was a chattering missile, falling faster and faster, ninety miles an hour, one hundred, one fifty, his eyes locked in on one of the grouse. If a grouse and the falcon take off at the same time, the falcon cannot necessarily catch the grouse by pure acceleration. The birds might get to speeds of eighty miles an hour like that, but from high stoop there is no contest. Miro was gaining on the grouse fast. The grouse was flying at top speed, having sensed that it was probably in the falcon's radar, but it had one advantage. An object traveling at eighty miles an hour can turn more quickly than an object traveling at one hundred and eighty. The grouse kept glancing back and up to see if it could find the attacker and knew that if it timed it right, it could make a quick turn as the falcon got close. Chances were, the falcon would go screaming past and have to brake to readjust, resulting in more of a fair fight once the grouse could go to ground or line out in the opposite direction. As it looked back and up, the grouse could not find the old falcon and almost seemed relieved. It became less frantic in its flying, perhaps thinking that the falcon had picked another target. Miro had learned that striking from one hundred eighty miles an hour took a toll on him as well. He learned to take the immense speed advantage and glide right under the grouse, right in its blind spot, still cruising at the speed of his descent. There seemed a moment when the grouse finally got suspicious and looked all around and finally down. There Miro's timing was perfect. In the space between the recognition of danger and doing something about it, there was enough room for Miro's talons. His powerful leg shot out sideways, his talons deep into the breast of the grouse. He tumbled with it toward the earth, then let it go so he wouldn't crash, curved up into the sky for a split second and dove down on top of the grouse to finish it.

 Griffin had been perfect. Robert called him in. By the time Sam got to Miro he was methodically plucking feathers off the grouse and flicking his head sharply to get rid of them, tossing a little storm of downy feathers up around his head as he prepared to eat his favorite parts. Even though they knew each other well, Sam moved in slowly for the last couple feet, walking on his knees to convince Miro to leave the grouse in exchange for some quail Sam had in his glove. With just enough trepidation to not to be taken for granted, Miro stepped off the freshly killed grouse onto Sam's fist. Once he was secure, Sam let Griffin carry the trophy grouse back to the truck. Both men glanced at each other, satisfied. This time it all went right, the way it should go. By the time Sam let Miro finish his well-earned meal and hooded him up the for the trip home, the sun was going down.

"Sam, I can't thank you enough. That was great."

"Maybe you and Maggie can come over for dinner. I've got enough now for a nice meal. Mind you I say that, but let me check with Jane. I never know what the girls are up to. Let's try for next Thursday."

"If it works, fine. I'll check with Maggie on the way home. Thanks again."

"It was fun," Sam answered. "I think he's going to be a really good dog."

The two trucks drove out of the bowl and when their headlights came on, they glowed like eyes, the only lights in any direction.

Once he hit Rt. 15, Robert called Maggie.

"Hi, did you ride? How did it go?"

It had been a good afternoon. The dog went well and her horse went well.

"Hey, I was thinking about dinner," he said. "I don't feel like cooking, do you?"

"Not really."

"How about if we meet at the Tavern in around forty minutes. We can get something there."

A little later, their vehicles simultaneously pulled into the crunching gravel parking lot in front of the old time western restaurant and bar. The doors closed soundly in the crisp night air. They kissed politely and Margaret went over to Sam's truck. She opened the door and roughed up Griffin's coat, talking sweetly to him and kissing him on the head. Robert stood there and muttered under his breath, "Maybe in my next life, I'll be the dog."

They had a pleasant conversation at a table near a large fireplace made of different shades of round river stones, reaching from the floor to the ceiling. He listened to another chapter in the endless academic politics and was already thinking of Thanksgiving. In their first years together, Maggie's father Augustine and his partner Johnny used to come out west for Christmas, but the travel just became too hard for him. With the flying and stress of the airports, the holidays seemed to become an all east coast affair.

"Maggie, do you have any idea yet of a schedule for going back east for Thanksgiving?"

"No, not exactly. I know we have to book tickets soon. It depends on how much work I have at school. I know you're not going to want to go for the whole week, but I think I would like to get there Sunday or Monday. You wouldn't have to come 'til Wednesday and we could fly back together on Sunday."

"You know we're going to have to go right back for Christmas."

"Bobby, I know," she said, half-apologizing, "but he's not going to be around that much longer. I'd like to spend as much time with him as I can."

"That's fine. I'll go Wednesday to Sunday, but I'll wait to book the tickets until you're sure. For the record, I think he's going to be around for quite a while." He meant it respectfully. She looked at him as if she wasn't sure.

Bob had married twice. He met his first wife, Eva Morrison, when he was finishing his residency in Chicago. He was wild into his work. She was a jealous woman and could not suffer the neglect his career seemed to demand. He didn't even argue when she wanted to leave. He just kept going. In the craziness of his patients, the creativity seemed unfathomable, the intrigue inexhaustible. He loved his work and he loved women. He wanted the same feeling from both. It was no accident that he was drawn to women who were a little unstable. In time, he began to wonder whether he was in love with a particular woman, in love with psychiatry or in love with the drug of irrationality and its relief from reason.

He met his second wife, Margaret Ogilvie Serano, when he had a job in New York. She was a psychiatrist like himself. Margaret's mother was Sandy Ogilvie, one of "the Ogilvies." Their family was once very wealthy, but generations of idle rich were eating up the carcass fast and no one seemed to be adding anything back. Sandy met Margaret's father, Augustine Serano, when she was a patient of his for a short time. Sandy fell in love with him and he was pleased by his new association with the Ogilvie's. They later married. Augustine became famous for some of his early work on psychotherapy and some seminal studies on memory. He published several books and had a department named after him at the Ivy League university where he was a member of the Board of Trustees. He was now in his eighties, but still had a practice in New York City. He would take the train in three days a week from the farm in the Catskills. His patients were a handful of old socialites and celebrities. He had lunch each day at the university club when he was in the city. It was as much because of his position as the times that Augustine kept his homosexuality concealed. For her part, Sandy knew he couldn't give her what she wanted. The truth was they both used it as an excuse. Augustine used it to escape the contradictions of his life by throwing himself into his work, which he would have done anyway. Sandy used it as an excuse to avoid work on why she felt so unloved and unworthy. Instead, she tamped that all down with alcohol, which killed her when she was still young. Still, they had a good relationship in some ways. They bought the farm together and seemed to love each other, but there was enough psychology in their two lives for ten troubled couples. Sandy died when Margaret was young. Maggie thought her father's lack of love killed her mother. The twist was that she thought it was her mother's fault. She was angry with her mother for not taking control of her life.

Augustine gave Margaret anything a child could want. He doted on her and coached her throughout her career. There wasn't a show horse that they ever bought together that could match the east coast pedigree of Margaret's education. Margaret and Augustine were very close, the balance of control and protection constantly changing. Augustine trained her to recognize power and that seemed to be enough to set off a natural attraction to it. She had all the tools to play the game. She was physically beautiful. She was smart enough to thrive throughout her elite education and she had enough family resources that she was never going to be hungry enough to snap at just any bait. She thought Robert was handsome and was even more impressed with his intellect. Although she might never be aware enough of it to deny it, she felt that wherever they went together, she would not be embarrassed by him. Margaret was so grounded, so in control, carried so much history that Robert felt like he was marrying up and into some order that he needed. It was time to grow up, he told himself. If there was a little electricity missing, maybe that was a good thing. In any case, it seemed to be more than made up for by their love of the outdoors: Maggie with her horses and Robert with his hawks.

CHAPTER TWO

The Meeting

Within two weeks, Marilyn Banks had contacted the Nelson's, arranged for a family meeting with Robert and had Sean's medical records sent to the clinic. Robert's office was comfortable, but not ostentatious. If younger children came in and saw large, dark leather chairs, they might be intimidated. He did have nice wooden cabinets built into the walls. Often, there would be children's games or art supplies lying around, but if teenage patients came in and saw coloring books they could be dismissive, so he kept all the props stored in the cabinets and could quickly change the stage if necessary.

Whenever he conducted first time family meetings, he always made sure there were enough individual comfortable chairs for each person, besides a long sofa. He liked to watch what configuration the family would choose when they sat down. He had his desk in the corner and a guitar out on a stand, but he only used the desk for work and never sat there during sessions. He always picked a seat after everyone else sat down. Marilyn buzzed him on the intercom to let him know the Nelsons had arrived. Robert checked the office over. Although he always had a pad of paper and some pens ready to jot down a question or an address, he almost never used them for that. More often than not he was sketching a picture or drawing something to help explain. He opened the door to the waiting room and introduced himself. Patricia Nelson was a small woman with reddish blond hair, wiry in frame and neatly dressed. Her mannerisms were a little on the quick side, but not like those of someone who was nervous; she was rather more like someone whose rhythms have been trained up by having too much to do every day. James Nelson was much taller. He had short hair and conservative clothes. It wasn't any stretch to see him as career military, yet his voice was pleasant, not so much in tone but in the absence of that kind of exaggerated formality and discipline that certain military people can have. Robert did not feel that he was standing next to a resting war dog. Sean was a cute kid. He was probably going to have his father's height and already had his mother's rosy hair.

"Please, come in. Make yourselves comfortable."

The Nelsons chose the sofa and Sean sat between his mother and father.

"Thank you for coming in. I know Sean has a brother and sister. I'm sure it wasn't easy to arrange the time to come in together. I think Sean's records have arrived, but I didn't want to go over them until we had a chance to meet and talk in person. So, maybe you can start at the beginning and give me a little sketch of the history."

"Well, Dr. McPherson," Patricia Nelson began, "I guess it started, or we noticed it, soon after Sean was born. James was deployed right after that. Richard, our oldest, was three. We were living in North Carolina. Both our parents lived in New York. They tried to come down and help me, and my sister would visit, but we didn't have much money. We are Christian and belonged to a church there. The people from the church were very nice. They would bring over clothes and food and checked in on me, but basically we were on our own. Everything seemed normal, but Sean started having sleep problems and then it developed into this strong separation anxiety. He couldn't be away from me. It was not the usual crying. He would get very upset. I tried everything, but Richard was still little and I didn't want to have him get sleep problems, so I let Sean sleep with me to calm things down. By the time James came home, Sean was a year old."

Robert looked at James Nelson.

"Mr. Nelson, what did you think when you came home?"

"I just thought it was normal. I was gone, he was an infant." James put his hand on Sean's shoulder and smiled at him, as if as gently teasing. "I thought she was going to spoil him."

"Well," she said, "to be honest, I thought the same thing. I must have encouraged it. Time went by and we had to move to Georgia. James was working a lot of hours. I had to deal with the kids. The biggest problem was the sleeping."

"Was it more trouble getting to sleep, or was it more during sleep?"

"During sleep. He had these night terrors. There was no consoling him. He can still have them."

Robert looked at Sean. "Sean, can you remember what was so frightening? I'm not asking you to tell me what it was. I just mean in general after you woke up, can you remember them?"

Sean shook his head no.

"Go ahead, Mrs. Nelson."

"Richard started school. Sean was alone with me and it seemed worse. He wouldn't let me out of his sight. I was at my wit's end, but somehow we were managing. Time went by and Sean was to go to kindergarten. James was deployed to Iraq. Richard was already in the small school, so Sean could see him every day and he knew he was there. For the half day of school, he seemed to be coping. Then there was an incident on a school trip. The school system psychologist asked us to come in because she thought Sean needed help. I was all for it, anything. I needed help. I didn't know what to do."

"Mr. Nelson, what did you think?"

"I agreed. When he was so upset at night it hurt. It was heart wrenching to see him like that and the screams were nerve wracking."

"Did Sean say anything during these vocalizations?"

"No, at least we couldn't make out anything."

"We started seeing a psychologist," Patricia Nelson went on, "who worked with a psychiatrist, and we started Sean on some medications, treating him for panic disorders and the sleep problems."

"What kinds of medications?"

"Anti-anxiety and sleep pills. I can't remember exactly what they were back then."

"That's ok. I can look that up. Did they help?"

"Yes, they seemed to help in that they calmed things down, but they didn't go away and he seemed to have no energy. That bothered all of us."

"What about cognitive behavior therapy?"

"Yes, but because we moved three times we saw new doctors and we would start all over again."

"There is no family history of seizures?"

"No," both parents answered.

"Sean, do you ever feel like you go off in a short daydream? Or that you kind of float off for a little while?"

"No."

Robert continued through what must have seemed to the Nelsons the most circuitous interview. At times, Robert seemed almost forgetful, coming back to the same question, repeating things; but he was masterful in interviews. He had learned never to ask questions in a predictable linear pattern. If people were consciously or unconsciously manipulating information, it was easier to catch discrepancies. In repetitions, the story might change or a new fact might come out. The more he talked to the Nelsons, the more things seemed relatively normal. No warning bells were going off; their body language was consistent with what they were saying. Sean seemed subdued, but that could be the meds. James Nelson had to deal with the typical problems of trying to have a military career and a family. Patricia Nelson seemed a little tired but who wouldn't be, running a marathon of child care every day with intermittent sleep. She didn't seem like the type to deliberately encourage this extreme dependence on her son's part, and she had two other children who had none of this behavior. Robert was now anxious to look over the records and read the thoughts of the other doctors. They had covered a lot of ground. Robert felt he certainly had enough information to begin.

"Ok, I really appreciate you coming in. I think it is very important to have family support and it seems you do. I would like to go over the records and then talk one more time together, at which point I could start seeing Sean. Do you have any problems with me talking to the other doctors or teachers?"

"No."

"Now, if I want to talk to you parents do you want me to call each of you individually, so you can hear directly from me? Obviously, I will if I have specific questions for one or the other of you or if you have special questions for me. But I'm referring to general updating."

"I don't think it's necessary to duplicate the calls. Pat will keep me posted. It's just simpler that way, with my job."

"I understand." Robert wanted to make sure they understood that the door was open and they could see him individually if anything came up. "Of course you can call anytime if you have questions."

They all stood up and shook hands. Then Robert asked James, "Mr. Nelson, you mentioned the sounds Sean makes, did they sound like anything you recognized? Any words?"

"One is very loud. It's a piercing scream like a hawk."

"A hawk, like bird of prey?"

"Yes."

"Huh. Ok, let me go over the records and we'll touch base once more so we can get started." He patted Sean on the shoulder.

It was Monday, and by Thursday night when Robert and Maggie were going to dinner at Sam and Jane's, Robert had reviewed all of Sean's medical records. It had been a hectic week. In the car on the way over to Sam and Jane's, they had each had their first chance to breathe. Robert was driving. He wanted to talk to Maggie about Sean Nelson.

"I have an interesting new patient."

"Oh?"

"A boy around ten, comes from a nice family, fairly religious. Father is in the military, so they have moved quite a lot. Mother is smart, they have three kids now. This one is the middle child. Problems were noticeable early. The mother described it as a kind of ultra-separation anxiety as a baby. They didn't have much money and the extended family were all in New York, so besides some help from the church, the mother was alone with the kids down south while the husband was overseas. She somehow was managing the child having pretty significant parasomnias."

"Nightmares, sleepwalking?"

"Night terrors, which I have to dig into more. When I asked him personally in the interview if he could remember the bad dreams he didn't say no, he just shook his head, which I attributed to shyness, but the parents corroborate. I'm wondering if they are too frightening for him to talk about or if they are classic terrors that he can't remember. The inconsolable part, the screams and violence seem to fit in with terrors. The mother managed the behavior until the kid went to kindergarten. It was a small school, his older brother was there so he could see him or knew he was around, so for a half a day he was holding on. Now comes the part where I have a question for you."

Maggie looked at him.

"Apparently the class went on a little trip to a zoo. I'm guessing some small local petting zoo. This child went over to a horse, which must have had a foal because it was lactating. He started either milking it or nursing from it, or both. The young teacher lost it, partially I'm sure from the danger, and partially from the oddity. I'm trying to reach that teacher and the school system psychologist they subsequently took him to see. In any case, it got blown up and the kid got tagged with a possible psycho-sexual diagnosis. Because the family keeps moving with the Dad, the kid has seen three different docs in the last five years. Two psychologists and one psychiatrist. The records are a bit all over the map, panic disorder, possibly hyperthyroidism or cardiac arrhythmias, although no evidence of family history. We've got separation anxiety, maybe depression, early onset psychosis, possible bipolar, of course all NOS. Then they start out with meds, from benzodiazepines to melatonin for sleep, to fluoxeltine, sertraline, paroxetine for the anxiety."

"Any cognitive behavior therapy during this?"

"Well, yes and no."

"Wouldn't that have been in order?"

"The problem was the moving. Just when the kid was ready, they would get a few sessions and something would happen and they would have to quit. Now the kid is ten years old. My question," Robert emphasized the 'my,' "is how this kid did not get his head kicked off by that horse? I wouldn't think of reaching up to the udder of one of your horses."

"Bobby, it's a petting zoo. These are animals that are selected because they are so safe. You said they are basically city people, living in army towns, suburban, but is the family from a rural background?"

"No."

"It probably just got blown out of proportion."

Robert felt as if she were patronizing him slightly. She seemed almost bored with his investigation. But he felt they were missing something important.

They were approaching Sam and Jane's, so they turned down the doctor talk. The girls were all home. As soon as they arrived, Jesse, the oldest at sixteen, wanted to show Maggie her new horse. Jesse was the only one with any real interest in animals. Carly, the middle girl, was fourteen and loved music. Sara, who was eleven, was very bright. Schoolwork was a breeze; she was very social and a bit obsessed with fashion. There was no way that one was ever going to stay in Montana. Sam and Jane had the cooking under control. The stone fireplace was crackling, resting dogs were scattered throughout the house. Sam was going to put the birds in for the night. As Jesse and Maggie came in the door from the stable, Sam and Robert went out.

Robert shook his head at Sam. "Busy place."

Sam looked at Robert as they walked toward the hawk house. "You know, there's a reason why in all sports there are the same number of players on each team."

Robert wasn't sure where Sam was going with this, but he kept listening.

"When we had Jesse, it was great. Jane and I could give each other breaks, cover for each other. It was two on one. There were some problems, but it was fine. Then we had Carly. It was still one on one. We had to up our game, but we were bigger and stronger than them and we had the money. When Sara came along, the whole dynamic of the game changed. We were outnumbered. If the other team has an extra player, it means that there is always one man open and defense turns to shit."

Robert was cracking up, laughing hard and trying to walk.

Sam looked at Robert, "And it's been that way ever since."

Inside the hawk barn, the three gyrfalcons stood on their block perches tethered with fairly short leashes. That way, if they bated, they couldn't get up enough speed to injure themselves. Miro was first, then a son of Miro and Nina, and then Nina. Robert was pretty sure Sam didn't remember that he knew the bird's real name was Santorina and that Robert was probably one of a very few people who knew she was named after a girl in Greenland who Sam fell madly in love with after a lonely summer there. He had been on his way home. As part of his work with the defense department, he could get free flights when they were available, back and forth to the arctic on cargo planes. The only problem was that the schedule was, well, flexible. He had met Santorina in a small village where he would pick up supplies and when he was to return to the States that summer, the plane was delayed. He had to wait two weeks. They were both unattached. They started drinking a little homemade immiak and for the next two weeks they were inseparable, falling into a heated affair. He tried to send her a letter after he left, but nothing came of it and the next summer he was off to Alaska. Obviously, he never forgot her. Robert respectfully never brought it up, but he knew a lot of people didn't really know Sam Lindley and how much he kept in a vault.

Robert kept thinking of Santorina the falcon. Santa Orina, he said to himself. If there were such a saint, it would look like her. A guardian angel, she would be at the gates of heaven. The front of her body was a study in white, except for the massive black talons beneath her white-feathered legs and the black tip of her strong, curved beak. The only other color was a brownish shadowing that helped with reflection under those huge, dark jewel eyes, uniform black pools that never seemed to emit emotion. He had to look at her body to see her mood, there were no clues in her eyes. Over her muscular shoulders, the feathers layered into the longest blades of the primaries on her wings, each scalloped in black bands. The study of her black and white markings reminded Robert of old paintings of English royals in white ermine trimmed coats. She looked regal and Nina had the personality to go with her looks. She was calm, never overreacting, and expectant of protocol. In the sky, she was fearless. She liked to rise so quickly and hunt from so high that it could be nerve wracking. This gave her astounding stoops, and with her heavier mass, they were all the faster, falling out of the sky. She rarely missed a target. Even if she overshot it, she was so strong she could catch almost anything if there was enough room to maneuver. Sam had talked about when he first trained her and he would call her from a fence post or perch a hundred yards away to his fist. He could see those glassine eyes, set in her pure white form, focus in on him. A few yards before him, she would drop a little and at the last moment pull her wings back and bring her talons up to bind to his fist. That was the drug, Sam said, it was a handshake with wildness itself. Sam had a pretty egalitarian view of all his hawks. They all had different skills and different failings, but all his intent toward intellectual equality was no match for nature's seductions.

When they got back into the warm house, Jane had prepared the grouse in a sweet, brown cherry glaze and had roasted what were probably going to be the last of the fresh fall vegetables. Maggie and Robert brought some of their favorite wine. Robert was always teasing the girls, and when they sat down to eat he noticed Jesse wasn't eating any meat. He glanced over at Sam. Sam silently shrugged his shoulders and lifted his hands carefully so Jessie wouldn't notice, as if to say, we've been over it, it's her decision, talk to her if you need to. Then Robert glanced over to Jane, pointing his eyes at Jesse's plate. Jane exhaled silently and gently lowered her eyes, but she and Robert both had slight smiles on their faces. The girls were not little children anymore. Robert felt the door was open.

"So, Jesse, I noticed you're not eating any meat …"

"Robert," Maggie intervened, "I'm pretty sure that is really none of your business."

"No, I'm a professional with children. It's ok." Robert looked at Jesse, waiting.

"I'm experimenting with becoming a vegetarian."

"Ahh!" he said, with just enough of a tone that he knew she would have to engage with him.

"You have an opinion," she answered with an equal amount of coyness.

"Jesse." With just the tone of her voice, Jane reminded her to be careful and polite.

Robert laughed. He loved to tease the girls. "Of course I have an opinion. I'm a man." Everyone laughed. "No, I really don't. Just make sure you get enough protein."

"We are." "I am." Jane and Jesse answered in stereo.

"Actually, I do have an opinion."

Maggie rolled her eyes.

"I've never had a problem if someone chooses to become a vegetarian because they feel it's a healthier diet. I do have a problem when people become vegetarians for moral reasons, meaning it is somehow morally ok to kill and eat plants but not animals. I like plants; plants like classical music. They respond to affection. Some of the oldest living things on the planet are plants. Which gets priority? A redwood tree that's thousands of years old or a rabbit? I get uncomfortable when people start making a list. We're really lucky today, we can choose our foods, but ask your Dad, that isn't normal. Mostly people ate what was available, what they had to. Do you know what haggis is?"

"No."

Maggie interrupted, "Oh no, Robert, not haggis again."

Robert kept going. "Well, it's chopped up heart, lungs, and liver of a lamb or cow." The girls reeled back in their chairs with disgust on their pretty faces.

"All packed and cooked in a sheep's stomach. It's all the parts that a poor Scottish farmer couldn't sell or no one else wanted. That's all they had to eat. It sounds disgusting, but I learned to like it from my father. I do really like it, but Maggie won't let me have it in the refrigerator."

Sam was laughing and the girls were cheering for Maggie.

"You mark my words, you'll come home from college one day and you'll ask your Mom to make something you learned to like growing up and your boyfriends will be aghast." Robert knew he had been on the soapbox long enough. "Sorry for the lecture, Jesse. It's just because I love you."

"It's fine," Jesse said, "but I think you should learn to unlike haggis."

Everyone laughed hard. Robert jumped up from his chair and went over to Jesse. From behind, he held her head in his hands and kissed her hard on the top of her head. He was practically shouting above the laughter.

"Well, I just might do that, but I'm not going to do it because of some fore-brain driven moralistic judgment. It would be because my cholesterol is too high!"

After dinner, Robert played the guitar while Carly played the piano. They promised to get together this year at Christmas to play and sing carols.

By the time Robert and Maggie got home, it was late. They were both tired. Before Robert got to bed, Maggie was asleep. It bothered Robert that though there always seemed to be good reasons, this was becoming more and more common. Before he fell asleep, he thought about the different women in his life. How they all started with that dance of ask and allow. The timing was so important, he thought. If he waited too long in responding to a touch, that space could seed insecurity and the waiting person might start to rationalize rejection. If he moved too fast or too hard, he could intimidate. There wouldn't be enough room for an answer, the response could be pressurized or worse, forced. In the beginning, almost anything could be excused when the hormones were flooding the brain. It was all so exciting, but coarseness didn't sustain that interest. There were likes and dislikes, more pleasure, less pleasure. To keep it alive, mistakes had to be explained as two people mastered living on the finest line between stimulant and irritant. Otherwise, people would quit and run. People give up so easily. People have to talk; if one asks the other has to answer. He and Maggie needed to talk, but it was as if he was trying to convince himself of something. What were they going to talk about? Didn't they already have these talks a long time ago? Why was he having doubts now, were things any different? Maggie hadn't changed; he could see her answers. He knew all too well the sear and the siren from a touch and from a touch ignored. As he fell asleep, he couldn't help but think of all the wrong choices he had made. Now he was having serious doubts as to whether he had grown up or was just growing old.

The next day, Robert finally got in contact with Dr. Josephine Graham. They had called back and forth and now Marilyn had her on the phone. Josephine Graham was the psychologist who first treated Sean Nelson after the horse incident.

"Dr. Graham, at last we make contact. Thank you so much for getting back to me."

"I'm sorry it took so long, Dr. McPherson."

"Please call me Bob, Dr. Graham."

"Everyone calls me Jo."

"Ok, Jo, thanks. Of course, you know what I called about. I'm not sure you'll remember the incident with Sean Nelson, but the family has moved here and they have asked me to help, so I am trying to understand the history. Do you remember the incident?"

"Yes, Bob, I do. Actually, it is fairly vivid, but I pulled some notes out to go over them to make sure my memory was correct."

"Do you think there is any benefit in my trying to reach the teacher who was there?"

"Of course that is completely up to you. She was pretty upset. I think she initially was shocked by her apparent negligence that had allowed one of her charges to get out of her sight and into a potentially dangerous situation. She was a young woman, quite conservative and a bit naïve; I think that later she let the strangeness of what happened relieve a little of her guilt, and she displaced some of the responsibility or blame onto the child for being disturbed. As I recall, we had some meetings at the school. The school nurse, the principle and I all had to be clear that these were personal and confidential matters and they were going to get professional consideration and that it was important that she edit her feelings and comments. She got the message. I wanted to start some cognitive behavior therapy and we – by that I mean the psychiatrist I consult with – decided to put Sean on some anti-anxiety medication after talking with his parents. The problem was, they were only here for about two more months before they moved. So I really didn't get into any therapy. I barely got to know Sean."

"Do you mind if I play the devil's advocate for a minute?" He was thinking of Maggie's attitude in the car when they had been going to dinner at Sam and Jane's.

"No, go ahead."

"Why was it thought that this might have psycho-sexual roots, instead of some insignificant petting zoo inappropriateness? A kid watches hours of TV, sees farm shows with cows being milked. Maybe he was showing off. All the kids could have been a little up from being out of school, inhibitions could have been down …"

"That's exactly what my thinking was when I first heard about it. But I had two problems. One was that if you have met Sean, you know he is no extrovert. He actually seemed mature for his age. Maybe a little nervous and tense, but he is no showoff. The second problem was that there were two cows next to the horse. He chose the horse specifically and he nursed milk out of the horse's udder like he knew what he was doing. I just didn't have an answer for that, but I was convinced it was not normal."

Robert was silent on the other end of the phone. He was absorbing what she had said and he felt a little presumptuous, questioning Jo Graham's assessment. When he spoke, he made sure he was extra polite in his tone.

"I see what you mean. Boy, I wish you could have worked with him."

"Yes, I do, too."

"I'm in a position probably not much different than yours. I've just met him and we'll have to see what happens. I think the family will stay here for a couple of years. Maybe we can get to the bottom of this. I really appreciate your time. If you ever get out this way for skiing or something, give me a call. Maybe we can have coffee."

By the middle of the following week, Robert had gone over Sean Nelson's records again and done a little more research. He set up a phone meeting with James and Patricia Nelson.

They both answered into a speakerphone.

"Hi, it's Bob McPherson. I just wanted to have a quick chat before scheduling a session with Sean. I reviewed his medical records. I think these are all well-meaning doctors you've worked with. I talked to a couple of them. I know it's obvious to you that there was no clear consensus among them as to what was going on with Sean. I think it points out that Sean's case is not clear-cut. Some disorders are relatively easy to identify; we can test and we have pretty specific diagnostic features that must be met or there are distinguishing symptoms. Asperger's, depression, ADD. But some blend or change over time. We have been making good progress using medication, but I personally am always trying to use the minimum dosage that will work. Of course, I would love to find a way not to use them at all." He could hear the Nelson's murmuring agreement.

"I don't know what the answer is or if there is one, but over the next few months we may decide to adjust the medications. Of course, I will talk to you if that comes up. I do think that if we are going to make progress, Sean is going to have to help show me the way. I think our sessions together will be very important, but it may go a little slow in the beginning until we get to know each other. I don't want to push too hard, but I promise I won't waste time, either. So, Sean and I can start with weekly sessions and I will meet with either one or both of you if anything comes up. However, Sean is going to have to be able trust me. I don't want him to feel that I will go running to his parents every time he confides in me. Do you understand what I mean?"

"Yes, Doctor. We agree."

"Great, do either of you have any questions?"

"What about the medications he is on now?" Patricia asked.

"I think we should leave everything the same for now. I will give you the necessary prescriptions at my office. Marilyn will come on the line after we're finished to make an appointment. Is there anything else?"

James Nelson spoke. "Dr. McPherson, at our last meeting you asked me about the sounds or noises that Sean makes. When we were in Indiana, the doctor there asked us to try to record those episodes, and we managed to do it. Pat and I weren't sure where it was since we moved here, but we found it. If you would like, Pat can bring it to Sean's appointment."

"That's great. By all means, bring it in.

CHAPTER THREE

The Sonogram

It all went wrong. Robert felt he should have known better. His falcon was too fat and the wind was too strong. All day long, the winds had been picking up. By the time it was his turn to fly, they were sailing. She got up in the wind and followed him and Griffin for a pass, but she didn't have her mind on the hunting. She rose a little higher and raked off out of sight. Now he was in his truck, barreling down the highway toward Julien, stopping every so often to scan the surrounding country, but the receiver was picking up nothing from the telemetry on the bird. He was being pretty hard on himself for obviously being more interested in socializing than in good falconry. They were interesting guys and he liked their company. For a long time, he had been making too many excuses why he couldn't go to this dinner or that meeting and they had planned this day months ago. He had known Sam wasn't going to make it since he had promised Jane and Jesse that he would go to Jesse's horse show. Robert had been busy at the office and knew he had not been flying the falcon enough, but it was a chance to cash in on some of his social debt. Now he was paying for it. It wouldn't be long before it was dark, he thought. It wasn't looking good. Then his phone rang.

"Did you find her?" It was Sam.

Robert felt embarrassed, but he was glad to hear Sam. "It was stupid. She was too fat, but I thought I'd give it a go. Goddamn it, how did you know?"

"Bill Clifford called me and gave me a heads up."

"That was nice of him."

"Where are you now?"

"Closing in on Julien. Everyone seemed to agree that with the prevailing winds out of the north, she would probably sail off in this direction. Down here closer to the lake, there are all the trees and ledges where I thought she might roost."

"I think you should turn around."

Robert was perplexed.

"By the time you get back to the cross roads, I can be there from here."

"Sam, you don't – can't leave the girls. It's not right."

"Jesse has already ridden. I need an excuse to get out of here! I'm so bored you'd be doing me a favor."

"Are you sure?" Robert tried to give him a way out, but he knew he could use Sam's help. Robert turned the truck around and started heading back in the opposite direction. He was half an hour from the crossroads. He wondered what Sam's thinking was. By the time he pulled into the gas station, Sam was there. He had a cup of coffee in his hand. He lifted it up and pointed to it, miming an offer of one for Robert. Robert motioned no thanks and Sam hopped into Robert's truck.

"So where are we going?"

"North."

"Ok." Robert pulled back out onto the highway, continuing north.

"How was the horse show?"

Sam sighed with half a smile on his face. "It was fine. Jesse is getting to the age where she's becoming more and more of an adult with her own ideas, so there's a little friction between her and Jane. I'm not sure she loves the horse thing, at least not Jane's idea of it. It's not a lot of fun. Kind of like refereeing."

Robert smiled. "You know, I think it's a great thing if a child shares a passion with a parent or parents, but over the years I've become more skeptical of most nepotistic interests. You and I know horse show mothers can be a force, but you see it everywhere. Soccer moms and Little League dads, the kids get a lot of reinforcement if they show the slightest interest in the parents' hype. Most of them do it because they see the joy in their parents' faces. It's like the infant making faces to make the parent giggle, not the other way around. For the most part it's harmless, but you know for some parents their hope can easily turn into design and a lot of kids I see feel trapped. The risk is that the kid can miss what they were supposed to do, they continue up the fish weir of their infused life and when they feel uncertain, they're told to work harder. If I make more money, if I get the promotion, then I will feel better. Christ, look at Maggie's colleagues. I think academics are the worst. Publish this, criticize that. They think that if they keep going, at a certain point up the ladder the view will clarify and a sense of completion will be there. So many miss it. Sometimes the chance for a kid's real life, the one for themselves, is a random connection. If parents fill up the kid's time, even if the intentions are good, there's no room for the kid just to wander around by themselves. Remember when you told me how you got into falconry, how that one neighbor had a bird and you were totally hooked? How many other falconers were there in that community?"

"None. There wasn't another in the whole town."

"Right, it was a slim chance. If your parents had your time booked, you might never have met that guy. I think a lot of times there is a statistically small chance. A radio show, a concert, for a kid there is that one chance event that can lead to a fulfilled life. In a strange way, I see more satisfied adults coming from slightly neglected, not abused, but not watched too carefully childhoods. Children's schedules today are ridiculous. Soccer moms are always bitching that all they do is drive. Who is forcing them? To me, there is a dual crime in these vicarious experiences. The kids get pushed into things they have no interest in, and the parent finds excuses why she can't pursue her own loves." Robert stopped himself. He glanced over at Sam. "I'm sorry for the running on. I'm kind of bringing the office home." The truck was cruising up the highway, which was pretty empty. They were probably halfway up to the country where Robert had last seen the bird. Off to the sides of the highway, the land was opening up even more. There were fewer trees, longer plateaus, nothing hiding the naked geology. Yet, in a strategic little notch of a valley or up against a hillside, there would be little ranches, tiny forts of civilization, miles away from one another. Robert caught himself taking it in, echoing against his own voice. "Jesus Christ, who lives up here? You and Jane are great. You've shown your kids stuff, but you haven't compromised on what is healthy for yourselves. That's a good example, not the way some parents raise their kids reminding them how much they've sacrificed so the kids can do what the parents couldn't. I've always thought that the difference between a mentor and a parent is that you find a passion and then a mentor."

He kept glancing out in the country at every pole and fence post where she might be roosting; it was automatic. "The passion is the guide. Parents find the child and start looking for a passion. The parent is the guide and they're not really good at it because they're often more concerned rightly or wrongly with keeping the child safe rather than self-actualized. Jesse is a strong-willed kid. You guys have raised her that way. Unfortunately, she's going to do what she has to do, even if it means disagreeing with her parents. You know, I can say all this because I don't have any kids, so of course I am an expert!"

They both laughed.

"Speaking of guides, where are we going, Kemosabe?"

"Unfortunately, you're not the only one to have lost a hawk up in that country."

Robert took his eyes off the road for a second and glanced at Sam's face, exaggeratedly raising his eyebrows without saying a word.

"Yes, twice. The first time, I went looking south like you did and I got a call from a friend who had gotten a call from someone who had gotten a call from someone and that someone saw a gyr. There weren't too many people flying gyrs, so I got lucky. The bird was up north. The second time, I went on a hunch against my own logic and again found the bird to the north. I would have agreed with you to look south if there was a cold front pushing in, probably any bird would use the winds, but I checked the weather and there was no front. These winds seem steady."

Sam lifted his arms and pointed low in all directions around them. "Since those times, we have done surveys all over this country in small planes." Now his arms went up, showing another layer. It was not just all sky or all atmosphere; to Sam it was as stratified and diverse as the earth below, but the sky could move so much faster. "The wind rushes down this valley, but when we got the plane up around a thousand feet or more, the wind would churn backwards, almost like an eddy from an oar going through water. So, the currents of the air are not as definite as they seem from the ground. Also, when you get up there and look toward Julien, there is some mining going on and I don't think the birds like the look of it. Who knows, maybe it was just luck."

It was almost dark. Sam had been scanning slowly in wide arcs, gliding the antennae across the landscape, when he thought he heard it or psychically felt it. He wanted Robert to slow down. There was a tiny, faint beep off to the north and west. It was the radio signal from the tiny transmitter on her leg. Robert's heart started thumping, he really liked that bird and he didn't want to lose her. They cut over to a side road and then onto someone's ranch. The beep kept growing stronger. Finally, in a huge cottonwood tree on the edge of a dried up creek, he could see her small, dark silhouette on a branch against the gray sky. Robert walked up carefully and whistled to her. He held out a tempting piece of quail, she cocked her head, he heard her bells as she moved her feet. She chirped and dropped off the branch. She curved in and out of the branches and glided to his fist. What a day. Robert sighed.

On the way back to the crossroads, they stopped at a small gas station and bought a six-pack of beer. They went outside and popped a couple open. They both leaned back against the grill of the truck and looked out at the country. Robert clanked his can against Sam's. "Thanks, man. What a day." It was particularly fine beer.

They just stood there for a little while. They were good friends. They didn't talk about it. They had known each other for so long, since kids, through all these phases of life. Even when they didn't see each other for long periods of time, all it took was a beer and it was as if no time had passed. One would look at the other, "You look well." The other looked back, "You look well," and it was as if there was no need to hear all the stories of what had happened in between. They sized each other up; they looked like they had survived and for now that was all that mattered. Today it had worked out. For the moment, they were just grateful to know each other.

As they were driving back home, Robert remembered the tapes of Sean Nelson.

"I have this new patient, it's a bit complicated but this person makes a sound and I have a recording. It is to me a perfect imitation of an eagle. The problem is there is no logical place where he could have learned this. I was thinking about having it analyzed to see if there was anything in there that might be informing."

Sam blurted out, "Birdman."

"Birdman?"

"Yes. Do you remember Joel Rubenstein from freshman year?"

"Oh, yeah, Birdman."

"Yes, he's still there. He's a big deal in Ornithology and bioacoustics. If anyone can help you out, he can."

"So just Joel Rubenstein, Department of Ornithology?"

"He'll be amazed to hear from you."

When Robert finally got home, it was late. He had called Maggie and she knew the story. She was still up. Robert was in the kitchen and Maggie walked in.

"So you found her?"

"Well, Sam actually found her. I'd still be looking," he mumbled, exhausted.

"Is she alright?"

"Yes, fine. Just some bad decisions on my part. Live and learn."

The whole time they talked, they stood almost ten feet apart, facing each other. He felt embarrassed, retelling the story wasn't helping. A touch would have been helpful; instead he felt like a child groveling at the edge of her shield.

"I'm glad it all worked out." She turned and walked out of the room. It was so hard to tell with her sometimes whether she lacked empathy or if she couldn't hide her distaste for any kind of failure. Robert was used to it. Inside, he shook his head. Jesus Christ, he thought to himself. He had no more fight left in him, at least not after this day.

"Thanks, I'll be up in a minute."

The next morning, Robert sent the recording off to Joel Rubenstein. He told him Sam recommended him highly and that he and Sam were both aware of his accomplishments, which was a little padded. The flattery couldn't hurt. It was good to be able to call on him. Joel responded the next day. He told Robert it was great to hear about them both. He would make a sonogram or spectrogram, he explained, to show how the voiceprint might look and so on. It might take a couple weeks as he was swamped with work at the moment.

It was two weeks to the day when Joel's information arrived. Robert had it up on his computer at the office.

Robert, the note read, *without going into too much detail, what you will see here is basically three graphs. I have included the sound so you can play the piece and watch it scan across the graph. What you'll see is a graphical representation of the video files. We've come a long way over the years. We can have pretty accurate representations of tone qualities, pitch, and timbre, plus we have algorithms that can filter out background noise like waterfalls in a jungle. We get a pretty clean result. The graphs you will see have time represented along the horizontal axis and frequency on the vertical axis. The intensity is color-coded and the chart is on the side. You'll hear it, of course. What you end up with is a kind of a voiceprint. I found your caller quite good and rather interesting. Your caller is represented in Graph A, it was a very good imitation of a North American Golden Eagle, which is Graph B. But then, out of curiosity, I did a scan of similar patterns, calls. If your caller does a very good imitation of a North American Golden Eagle, he or she does an even better imitation of a Golden Eagle from Kazakhstan. Our recording came from falconers who were studying the Mongolian, Asian, Tibetan and*

Chinese hunters who still use eagles. I hope you find this useful. It was good to hear from you. Keep in touch. Best, Joel.

Robert leaned back in his chair and played them over and over. He wasn't sure he could hear the differences, but the graph was very clear. He leaned back again and clicked repeat a couple more times, listening, thinking.

Chapter Four

Sean

Robert had about run out of tests. He had started seeing Sean, but in order to be sure his dreams, terrors or hallucinations were not caused by petit mal seizures or some rare form of Rasmussen's, he had to check for epilepsy. The EEG and CT scan had come back normal. Robert played it by the book, trying to come up with a diagnosis: anxiety disorders, conduct disorders, panic disorders, pervasive developmental disorders and every co-morbid combination he could apply. He knew many of his colleagues would just go ahead and treat the symptoms, understanding they might never know the cause and some even arguing that the cause doesn't matter, but Robert wasn't at that point yet with Sean. If he were forced to offer some kind of diagnosis, he would say that Sean resembled someone with Post Traumatic Stress Disorder, but if there was trauma it wasn't obvious. He knew he had to be careful, what if Sean had suffered some kind of trauma and it was a result of some kind of abuse? Robert had to find out. Was it one major incident? Was it multiple incidents, and the most important question of all, was it still going on? Sean hadn't really been in any situation where some caregiver could have traumatized him without his parents knowing, which led to a more ominous question. Did they know? It had to be considered. Robert had been around master manipulators and the last thing to do was underestimate their skills. In a perverse way, he had to appreciate the skills they were forced to learn as children because they were abused and became savants at reading the slightest moods, to forecast. They mastered distractions that might postpone more trauma, and if all else failed the mind might dissociate, the brain flooding the system with opioids, numbing and anaesthetizing, distancing from the reality of the inevitable, anything to try to survive. Then, there was the fear that if they did survive, they might use their skills to hurt someone else. The person causing the pain to the person Robert was treating now could have been the person Robert was treating fifteen years ago. Robert knew too many cases where one spouse might not have any idea what their partner was truly doing, or if they had a clue they were in some complicated denial. Unless he was completely missing something, Robert didn't think this was where Sean's trauma was coming from. His parents would not have repeatedly sought help for him at the risk of exposing themselves. By now, Robert had had several interactions with them both and there was nothing to lead him in that direction, but Robert had learned a long time ago from Archie not to trap himself in his own self-impressed deductive web. Turn it upside down, he would remind himself, especially when he felt certain. Sean was going to have to help. Robert was feeling more and more that Sean's terrors were not classic night terrors that Sean could not recall. He was feeling the silence about them was now habituated. Maybe it started even before he could talk, so he suppressed them. He certainly didn't want to voluntarily bring them back up, although Robert seemed to be convincing him that they kept coming back up anyway so the strategy of trying to push them back down wasn't working very well.

"Hi Sean. So how was your week?"

"Ok." Sean rambled on a little bit about school, nothing dramatic. Whenever Sean came into the room by himself, Robert knew he wasn't alone. Robert had developed an almost instinctive reflex reaction to phrasing and voice tones. Mostly though, he felt he could smell the filters of the drugs. He knew their effects so well, they seemed like personalities of themselves to him. They made him feel like there was a ghost in the room, minders who kept him from getting to know the real person. He was like a lot of his patients. He liked drugs and he hated drugs. If almost any parent lost a child, there would be no amount of wealth, power or pleasure they would not trade to have their child back.

Joy and pleasure always seemed temporary and were not equal opposites of sorrow and pain. They were lighter, they were a bonus. Pain was much heavier ounce for ounce, but Robert had seen time and time again it was not that simple. A life with no happiness or pleasure was not much of a life. To cling, to enable, to be motivated by guilt hurt more than the one sick or injured person, it was malignant and it spread to a community of people. The art of his job was to try to find some way to balance the filters, but he always knew when the bodyguards were in the room.

"Sean, the last time you were here we started to talk more about the things that make you uncomfortable or fearful, do you remember that?"

"Yes, I think so."

"Now, your father is a soldier and it can be a dangerous job being a soldier. When you were first born your Dad was away in a dangerous place."

"Iraq."

"Yes, he was gone. It would be normal to be afraid he might not come home. I know you were probably too young to remember the first time, but when he went back again, and later to Afghanistan, certainly your Mom would have worried about that. I'm sure she still does. Does that or did that ever bother you?"

"Maybe, but not so much anymore because he's not going to go to war."

"Your Mom and Dad said you would wake up and be pretty upset. They said you would have headaches. You told them it felt like there was a claw in your head, do you remember any of that?"

"Yes, it can still happen."

"The pain, the fear or both?"

"All of it."

"Has it happened recently?"

"If I take the medicine it helps."

"It used to upset you quite a bit if you were left alone. What bothered you or still bothers you about being alone?"

"I think about scary things when I'm alone. They come into my mind."

"Are you afraid someone you know would not return or they would die?"

Sean looked at Robert, slightly annoyed.

"Are you still talking about my father?"

"Not necessarily. I'm wondering what the scary things are that come into your mind?"

"Little kids can get hurt when they are all alone."

"How? What kind of hurt?"

"They can be killed." Sean was getting upset. Robert tried to calm him down, but he wanted to get a little further. He asked Sean if he was afraid of death. Sean was getting agitated, but he wanted to try to tell Robert.

"It's like a dream that comes back over and over. It's the end of the world. It's all black. Even if I die, there is no one else that stays on living. My brother, my sister are gone, there are no more people, no animals, nothing. It's all gone. It's just a black, cold space that goes on forever."

Sean was visibly shaken. Robert thought they had gone far enough. He started to bring Sean back, but his attention was divided. He was trying to memorize and process what Sean had said, but he was also trying to settle things down. Robert was a little baffled, this kid came from a pretty religious family, a Christian family. He had been going to church every week since before he was born. He attended Bible study classes, but there was no mention of heaven or hell, no fear of the devil or thoughts of Jesus Christ, not a word about God or any of the teachings about life after death that Sean must hear every day. Instead there was a nihilistic portrait of empty, cold fear itself.

"Sean, this is very helpful. Thank you for talking about that. I know it's not easy. You are very brave. I think for today that is enough. I want to show you something that is useful for anxiety and nerves aside from medication. I use it myself to gain control of racing thoughts. It's a breathing exercise that lots of people in martial arts and athletics use. It's a basis for meditation."

Robert went to the cabinet.

"Do you know what this is?"

"No," Sean shook his head.

"It's a heart rate monitor. I'll show you how it works." Robert put the heart rate monitor on Seam and attached a little read out like a wristwatch. "If you press this button, you will hear a beep that corresponds to your heartbeat, and the number on the screen is the number of beats per minute. Really fit athletes' resting pulse rate will be quite low. For children your age normal is 85 -90 beats per minute."

Sean was well over one hundred; he still had not calmed down.

"Press the button again to turn it off for now. I'm going to show you how with a breathing exercise. You can use it to help center yourself and calm yourself down. Do you want to try it? It's simple but it takes a lot of practice."

Sean was fascinated with the toy-like qualities of the device.

"These breathing exercises are very old. You can sit cross legged." Robert showed him.

"Or, you can kneel and kind of rest on your heels. I prefer to be on my heels, it's more comfortable to me. You want to be comfortable. Not like in bed, but not in pain. You'll have to experiment and see which way you like better. Let's start with the kneeling one. Now you inhale through your nose. You can think and listen to the sound of the air being pulled through your nose into your lungs. Make it last as long as you can. Not so deep you feel like you are going to burst or cough, but slowly. It takes practice to keep your attention on your breath. Then exhale through your mouth. Think of the air flowing out and listen to the sound. Feel it low in your stomach and again through the nose. You have to keep thinking of the breathing, inhale, exhale. You want to try it?"

"Sure." They both sat on the floor.

"Ok, turn on the heart rate monitor. What does it say? Now forget it, let's go." They both began to breathe like a couple of monks. Within a very short time Sean's heart rate started going down. Robert waited a little bit and then gently tapped Sean. With his finger up to his lips to remind him to stay quiet, Robert pointed to the monitor. Sean smiled with his success.

"In time, you won't need this, but for now we're going to use it to help you learn," Robert whispered. "Keep breathing."

Robert quietly got up, listening to Sean's breaths getting longer. He picked up a brand new tennis ball and then he threw it over Sean's head, pretty hard. It bounced off two walls. Sean almost jumped off the floor and looked at Robert as if he were crazy. Robert smiled and pointed to Sean's monitor – it was racing. He caught the tennis ball and handed it to Sean with its bright yellow brushy cover, like the coat of some little animal.

"How are we going to handle attacks of anxiety when a cute little yellow ball sends your heart through the roof?"

Sean laughed.

"Sorry for the fright. I won't do that again, but you see my point. That's why I said it was simple. You were successful right away, but it's also difficult, look how quickly and easily you lost it. I'd like you to try every day for a few minutes. Use the monitor. You can take it home. Next week is Thanksgiving. I have to go out of town so we will miss a session, but when I get back I want to see how you're doing with it. Remember, inhale, exhale, through the nose, through the mouth, no interruptions. After ten minutes check your heart rate, write down each day the beginning and ending rates. Anything that comes into your mind let it come and go. Don't hold on to it. Just keep focused on the breath, ok?"

"Ok."

"I think your mother is here to pick you up."

Robert buzzed Marilyn on the intercom and asked if Patricia Nelson could come in. He explained the monitor and what he wanted Sean to do. He gave them extra batteries and apologized for being out of town the next week.

CHAPTER FIVE

Back East

Maggie was already at the farm in Warfield, New York with her father and Johnny. Robert took care of some last minute details and drove himself to the airport in Missoula. It was very early and still dark. The singular sound of his pickup door shutting echoed through the quiet parking lot. As he walked in the cold, clear November air toward the terminal he took a deep breath. In a few hours, he would be in one of the busiest airports, in a different world. He had talked to Maggie and the plan was for him to fly into New York and take the train to Warfield, the same train Augustine Serrano had taken every Tuesday, Wednesday and Thursday for fifty years. Thankfully, the weather looked good for travel, nothing dramatic for the whole holiday weekend. Robert had only a small carry-on roller suitcase for the couple of days. He was the first person through security. There was no one behind him. It would be a little different trying to come back from New York. He must have picked up a little stone in the parking lot because the one wheel of his suitcase was stuck. He went upstairs to his gate. The escalator was not working so he hitched the luggage case up the motionless, toothy stairs. Up near his gate, he bought a cup of coffee. There were no delays and before long the small jet was lifting off for Salt Lake City, where he would connect for New York. Robert liked the actual flying, especially the take offs and landing in daylight when you could see the country from a falcon's perspective. To travel above all the impediments of geography was sublime. A bird steps off a rock and opens its wings and with a few strokes, like an Olympic rower, levitates to a desired altitude. A man climbs the stairs of a broken escalator dragging a suitcase. What can you say? From Salt Lake, the plane was full. It was of course one of the busiest weekends of the year for travel. People struggled with too much luggage. Veteran travelers endured, sinking deep into themselves, wondering what went wrong with the schedule. Neophytes talked too loud, too fast and too friendly, trying to cover their excitement or anxiety. Vacationing couples were stressed, reading and rereading their departure times and gate numbers to each other until one of them lost patience and infuriated an air hostess by tapping her on the rump as she went by, trying to ask her an unanswerable question. Once the plane crossed the Mississippi, there were no more vast, empty tracts of land. It was all cultivated, squared, rounded, blocked-in human geometry. For some strange reason, Robert remembered a scene when he and Margaret were dating and she took him to see the estate of her mother's uncle, Francis Reeves Ogilvie, which had been turned into a museum of antique American furniture and textiles. It was an impressive place, big enough that there were little surrey kinds of shuttles with open sides that toured the grounds on the way from the cafeteria and gift shop to the house. The guide was a retired high school teacher who loved his job. He had his speeches so perfectly memorized that they seemed to appear spontaneously at various noteworthy sites along the way. There was room in them for his light sense of humor. The little bus passed the pinetum and then the oldest cherry tree in America and then the appropriately named South Glen, where a massive garden of seemingly wild rhododendrons were naturally maintained by more than one PhD from some agricultural college. Then they went through Maristan Wood, a few acres of stately, huge tulip poplars and beeches where the guide had another anecdote about Francis which was crafted to make him sound more ordinary than a man who lived for thirty years in an American castle until he died.

Paul Belasik

A man on the shuttle asked "Terrence" if the "wood" was virgin timber. Terrence in his perfectly mannered voice, estate-trained, no question is ever too stupid, I'm here to serve you, the public, and be your friendly guide, politely told him that was not possible, which seemed to translate to everyone else.

"Shit, man, are you kidding? This is the East Coast! We're roughly fifty miles from Manhattan. There is no virgin anything here, and this is probably the third or fourth time these trees have tried to grow back since Plymouth Rock."

So, Robert was in a good mood though his senses had to sink a little to handle the overload as he walked up the tunnel jetway, which emptied into the cacophony of one terminal, which led into a more cacophonous terminal and so on. All the races of the world seemed to be represented. He was glad he didn't have to stay there and connect to another flight. He only had to make his way to a shuttle, which took him to the train station. It wasn't long before he was on the train. He had gotten a seat by a window. The train began creaking out of the station past the graffiti-covered abutments and the backsides of random apartment buildings and warehouses. It passed the miles of filthy chain link fence that was supposed to protect the trains and tracks from people or people from the trains and tracks, but instead stuck out like some great dredging fish net pulled up into the air with its catch of beer bottles hanging halfway up by their gills, plastic bags caught inflating with the wind like blowfish, and some occasional mattress or sofa bending the fence with its bottom-feeding halibut weight. Yet, as dense and ugly as the city was, it was amazing how soon real rock cliffs, not concrete buttresses, began to appear with little streams dripping down, already forming ice outcrops. Cedar trees and hemlocks appeared, growing out of the rock crags and in no time little farms started appearing, then some bigger ones with ponds full of geese. The ancient mountains were low and rounded. Most of this country had passed its prime when it was once a playground and escape for wealthy New Yorkers who sent their kids to camps up here in the summer, where they had cottages on lakes with Indian names or where they owned working retreat farms. There were still a few pockets of neat, manicured communities. Wakefield was one of horse country.

Maggie picked up Robert at the train. She had her hair up, she had been riding. In fact, she had been riding every day. She was waiting on the platform when Robert's train pulled up and Robert got off. The train was fairly crowded and a dozen people got off at Warfield. He saw her and walked over to her. They kissed.

"Are you exhausted?"

"I'm ok." He never understood how you could get so tired apparently just sitting for a whole day, but he was.

"I'm parked over here."

She led the way over to the gravel parking lot. Her car wasn't more than one hundred feet from the little station. Robert tossed his bag into the back seat and sank down into the passenger seat, up front. Maggie turned the car on and backed it up. She looked behind her, then to the side. Her head moved quickly, but she never looked at him. He noticed her hair. He liked it up, but then he just stared forward out the windshield. She pulled out onto the main road.

"Do you think you are up to having dinner a little later at the Inn? Daddy and Johnny won't want to be out late. Johnny will be cooking all day tomorrow, so no one feels like cooking tonight."

"That's fine."

She asked about Montana. He answered. It was all polite small talk, but they seemed to let down their guard. Maybe she was more relaxed up here, he thought. By the time they got to the farm, they were laughing about something. Why, he wondered, was there always that standoffish posturing to start with? Maybe it was as much his fault. But it wasn't getting easier, he always fet he had to break down a wall to get started. Sometimes it was easier just to look out the window. He didn't want that.

In was dark when they drove through the stone pillars that marked the entrance to the farm. The long drive curved around so that the house was not visible until the second big curve. They had to drive slowly because there were deer all over the place, especially after dark and because Augustine would not pave the road or make it too easy for people to drive fast. His concession every few weeks was to get Raphael to hook up the clamoring, heavy steel drag to the tractor and screech it down and back, grinding the stones on the gravel road, leveling the worst pot holes, creating on a dry day a column of dust that rose like smoke from a forest fire. Johnny would run around the house, slamming all the windows shut, swearing about the dust. When they rounded the second bend, there was the stone house with little glittering candle lights in all the windows. It was one of the oldest farms in Warfield. A long, low matching fieldstone barn stretched out behind the house across a cobblestone courtyard. It was set in a mild valley that sloped up to a small old mountain behind the house. Augustine owned this side of the mountain. It was just trees and some trails for horses. There were no buildings, no lights. The compound seemed remote, a medieval outpost. It reminded Robert of Scotland.

Augustine and Johnny seemed glad to see Robert. Robert thought Augustine was beginning to show his age. Johnny had put on a little weight, but still looked pretty fit. Johnny Crane was about ten years younger than Augustine. He had moved in with Augustine a few years after Sandy died. They had been together for twenty years. Augustine called Johnny the mayor of Warfield, because Johnny seemed to know everyone and everyone seemed to know Johnny. Johnny had no time for pomposity, his wit could be a weapon, but he cared about people. If he heard a sad story at some party or at a bar, he would listen, often not saying much. But in a couple of days that person might get a note from him or a visit. He'd had a couple of ideas. Here's a phone number of a friend of mine, give him a call. I think he can help you. Everybody owed Johnny favors. It wasn't that he was wealthy or socially connected in his early days, but as he would say, everybody needs a friend sometimes. Over a lifetime an impressive list of people grew and grew. He never asked a favor for himself. Everyone felt that if he called, it was a compliment. He might be stumped but he thought perhaps you knew enough about this subject or that to help out a friend, maybe just some advice. People were happy to do it.

Johnny had one sister. Their father had worked his way up as a teenager in a textile business from a stock boy to vice president. When his father died, Johnny was in his forties working sporadically in New York with an advertising business. He would rather be riding his horse, so he worked a few days on and off. About a year or so after his father died, Johnny's mother thought it was time to sell the house and get into an assisted living arrangement. Johnny thought it was a good idea. They researched some places and found a nice one that everyone liked, close to the old neighborhood. With the money from the sale of the home just outside New York and a generous pension, Alicia Crane was in good shape and was enjoying life with her cronies in the community. Sometime later, she was putting the finishing touches on her estate. She had a feeling she wasn't going to last long. Johnny got a call from her. She told him Father had planned out everything before he died, he had told her to sell the portfolio of stocks as she needed to. He had told her that their old broker would help and if he died there were several people back at the company who could be trusted to help, but he told her to hang onto the company stock and to sell the other stuff first. The company stock had sentimental value. Alicia thought there was no point in just keeping it anymore, since she wanted to get her own finances in order. Did Johnny think Father would mind if she sold the stock? Johnny was washing dishes and he held the phone between his cocked head and shoulder.

"No, don't be ridiculous," he said, "Dad would have wanted you to. This is what he meant to save it for. How much is a share worth?" he asked her.

"Around forty-six dollars," she answered.

"How many do you have?"

"Twenty thousand," she answered, matter of factly.

The next sound was Johnny's phone falling into the sink water. Alicia died the next year. Johnny and his sister each inherited a cool five million and Johnny never used the word boss again.

He and Augustine were a good match. Augustine was smart. He knew his life was too much show and costume, but he became addicted to accomplishments. He would let them define him even though deep inside he didn't trust them, especially new ones. They were hard to control. So he had been doing the same work for a very long time. His motto was to fortify, and then fortify the old work some more. His stone house, the great stone building of the university and the hospital complex, all that stone was no accident. They weren't moving. There was history there. If sometimes it was inaccurate, that was irrelevant. In the stone, power was consolidated and power would generate ideas. The greater the walls around some prestige, university or hospital, the more he needed to be inside them and the more he would defend them. He coached Maggie through her career more relentlessly than any horse show mother. He wanted her back here. He loved it when she was home. Johnny tempered all of that. He couldn't stop Augustine, but he calmed him down.

Robert took a shower and dressed. They all drove off to the Inn. The Inn was a historic stone building set along the river. Inside it had rich wooden paneling and candles. Most of the building was original from the colonial days, but any part that had been restored was done artistically. Tables with deep green cloths surrounded by worn Windsor chairs were situated near the thick stone windowsills that looked out toward the river. At one end of the dining room, there was a massive stone fireplace. There was a separate bar room with a magnificent back bar of chestnut wood and mirrors that was expertly stocked. As they made their way to their table, every waiter and waitress acknowledged them. Johnny seemed to have a brief question for each one, a serious one about someone's health in one family, a teasing one about someone's new romance. They sat down, ordered some drinks and in minutes Augustine and Johnny's identical martinis arrived with Robert and Maggie's wine. The conversation turned to the big dinner tomorrow. Johnny insisted that he had everything taken care of, but Maggie and Robert both told him that after the morning they would both be available for the rest of the day. Of course Johnny wouldn't hear of it. Robert told him he would go out for a run and then he could wash dishes. Johnny begged them to stop and finally conceded he would find them something to do.

The meal at the Inn was excellent and true to their word, they didn't stay very late.

In the morning, Robert went out for a run. It was cold, but still too early for any serious snow. Out west, this temperature would seem easy to tolerate, but with the humidity here he wanted to get moving. He started off down the lane through a section of woods. The last salmon colored leaves of the smooth silver beech trees hung on, but all the other trees were now bare. It was easier to see around and to tell the trees apart. The hickories had shaggy, splintered bark and the maples all had rings of holes in them, the sites of taps where someone had collected the sap for syrup in the early spring. A house he never noticed was now plainly visible as well as the ridgelines of the rounded old mountains. He picked a side road. The stone walls went on for miles, from the squared and manicured walls around houses and barns to the casual piles that outlined the pastures and croplands of the hill farms. The Dutch and English who settled a lot of this land after routing the Native Americans left a legacy of simple stone architecture. Some had become huge estates, homes with carefully landscaped gardens and lawns wrapped around lakes with swans in them. Other lakes were filled with Canada geese seemingly stalled in their migration because of the good eating. Horses in blankets dotted the still green pastures. After a couple of miles, Robert took a road that turned toward the village. There a certain reality struck as he passed a few broken down houses with jalopies parked near them at odd angles and then some trailers and a tiny Mexican restaurant. Americans had become too spoiled to work on the horse farms but Mexicans would come legally or illegally and a symbiosis developed between horses and the Mexicans: moral, tireless workers who fed them, groomed them and mucked their stalls everyday throughout America. Liberal politicians, conservative politicians, Ivy League professors, lawyers and their wives or husbands lived on manicured farms cared for by Mexicans who were often paid cash. It was a quaint feudalism. Everyone had their own municipality. At least on the Serano municipality there were no illegals. Susan was the barn manager and there were Mexican workers, but Augustine only let her hire legals and he personally knew them by name.

Robert crossed the river that ran through the little town and ended up on the other side of the river from the Warfield Inn. From there, the Inn looked like some monastery in Tibet. The stone work of the buildings was woven into the natural cliffs so perfectly it was hard to tell where the buildings began or where the cliffs ended. In time, he jogged back in between the stone pillars that marked the driveway into the Serano farm. Robert walked the last half-mile to the house. It wasn't as palatial as some of the places he had passed, but it was tasteful, stately, and it had character. It was just right for an Ogilvie couple a few generations removed from Francis's palatial lifestyle. Robert walked into the kitchen where Johnny was already at work on the big meal.

"Hey Bobby, how was your run?" he put his hands on his stomach. "I should have been out there with you," he laughed. "What can I get you for breakfast?"

"I have to settle a bit and take a shower. Besides you have enough to do. I'll get something myself."

"It's no problem, really."

"Thanks." Robert went to the sink and drank a couple glasses of water, and then got a cup of coffee to visit with Johnny for a bit.

"So, have there been any offers on the farm?" Robert asked, a little facetiously.

Johnny looked back at Robert, rolling his eyes sarcastically. It was all but a running joke that Augustine would finally agree to sell the place and they would find something they could retire to.

"There is no way anyone will buy it for the price he is asking. This way he placates everyone, but in reality it's conveniently off the market. He thinks we're immortal. Bobby, the place is too much. Every time it rains, the stone around the windows leak. There are things everywhere that need to be done. We're old. We used to be able to do some of this stuff before, but it's unrealistic now. We could drop two hundred and fifty grand into this house and you wouldn't even see it. This farm needs new blood, a transfusion, that's what it really needs, but he's an icon in a town full of icons. You know how much effort in takes for him to maintain that façade. That is probably what keeps him going so strong. Icons have to have horse farms. You can't remind people of your power from a condominium. I tell him, Auggie, you never even rode. I haven't ridden in years. What are we doing this for? He'll tell me things like it is wealth and power that give ideas force and I remind him that before he had any power his ideas were the force. Bobby, you and Maggie should move back here. He'd give you the farm. That's the only way he'll leave standing up. Maggie would love it."

Robert sighed. He had heard all this before.

"You know, he's got this scheme that Maggie should be the next Dean of Psychiatry at the University here."

"No, I didn't know that," Robert wasn't surprised. Augustine always had ideas for Maggie's career. Robert had stopped paying attention to them all.

"It could be perfect," Johnny sang the phrase, tempting with his voice, teasing that Robert and Maggie could be his way out of the place. Robert laughed. He knew Johnny, knew how he felt, but Robert knew he couldn't live on a place where he felt he would have to spend so much time and effort sculpting appearance and maintaining image. Robert had mixed feelings about Augustine. In some ways, especially because he was in the same field, he admired his achievements. Yet at the same time, he wondered what was behind them. It was time to change the subject.

"Speaking of Maggie, is she riding?" Robert walked over to the window and looked out toward the stable.

"Yes, they're in the indoor school. He likes to sit up in the balcony."

"Ok, I'll leave them to have some time together. Let me go get a shower and I'll come and help you."

"Bobby, Bobby, do you see that pad of paper over there? It's a minute-by-minute plan of my day. I've got it covered. If I get too much help the meal will be all fucked up."

"Ok, I'll wash dishes."

"Go take a shower. We'll see."

Augustine sat up in a viewing room open to the riding arena. He was wrapped in a big robe to keep warm. Robert knew how much he loved watching Maggie ride. Was it the aesthetic beauty or some kind of pride laced with fear, watching her gracefully control the large, powerful animal? Augustine could never in a million years get up on one of those beasts, much less gallop it over fences, stone walls and streams. He never had that kind of courage. He must have secretly wondered how she could do it, not just as his daughter, but as a human being. She wasn't oblivious to the danger. How did she overcome it? His age was showing. Even though it was morning, the rhythmical pattern of the horse's hooves in the muffled footing would be hypnotizing and he would probably have to fight dozing off.

Robert showered and changed and went downstairs to try to help Johnny. Augustine was already in the kitchen, sitting on a chair. Then Maggie came in, and Johnny chased them out into the living room. He would need help in an hour, he promised. Robert couldn't help watching Maggie drape herself over a big leather chair. She looked so good in her tight riding clothes. He knew she would look even better in the dress she was going to wear to dinner. She fit in that room, he thought, she fit in that house, but she always dressed for style and not for provocation, entertainment or pleasure. To him, it seemed like such a waste.

Maggie had grown up as an only child in an unusual family. When she and Robert first started dating, Robert tried to talk to her about her childhood. He couldn't understand how Augustine seemed blameless to Maggie. He could understand the trauma effecting a child whose mother essentially committed suicide, but Augustine was a psychiatrist, for Christ's sake. Why didn't he correct the kid or get someone who could? For two psychiatrists, it was incredible how unanalytical the conversation between Robert and Maggie had been. She would almost get angry with him. "Why the probing? I've told you the story. It's sad but it's not that complicated. My mother couldn't control her drinking, she couldn't control whom she loved and that lack of control killed her."

Gyre

For Robert, it wasn't that simple. He thought it was lack of love that killed her, not lack of control. And, if someone thought love needed all that control, maybe they were incapable of it. But that discussion was never going to take place outside of Robert's own mind. Although it seemed to be a hot, steamy psychological bayou, maybe it wasn't. Maggie had a long history of making decisions quickly, easily. She rode her horses like that. Once she made her mind up, it was irrevocable. She seemed hard wired that way. Afterwards, there was no new evidence admitted, the case was closed. Maybe it was closed for Maggie and Augustine, but how could it go away for Robert? He lived it every day. It was no wonder she didn't show affection. Where would she have learned it? Ideas can't be substituted for touch. It had affected the development of her own physical desires. She transferred that energy to an intellectual plane. It was how she wore clothes: perfect style, perfect taste on a beautiful body. But it was for the mind, not so much for touch. Of course, Augustine was all encouraging. He could show off her beauty and never had to worry about teenage sexual transgressions. He never asked himself if this was right for her. He felt so good about it for himself. He thought he was just lucky when he compared his daughter to some of his friend's children. Maggie grew up satisfying her sensual needs with the feel of horses, the excitement of speed and power, wind on skin, the friendship of dogs. The finer, deeper needs she satisfied with her mind. There was another problem, though. She may have felt she handled her own desire but when a woman looked the way she did, it wasn't only up to her. She may have wanted to deny her looks had anything to do with her place in the academic world, or the way people approached her, smiling at her all the time, trying to be her friend, but it was what caught Robert's attention. Now, as she lay in the chair, he thought that there were irresistible forms, combinations of senses, sights, sounds, tastes, scents. An orchid, a falcon, saffron, jasmine, a musical phrase that would make you stop whatever you were doing. To understand these things was to let them have their effect, to let go and enter that sensual world. Robert had been trying since they had first met to fall into Maggie, but she wouldn't let him.

Augustine broke Robert's concentration. He began telling Robert that there was a real chance Maggie could be the next Dean at the university. Robert glanced at Maggie. He had heard this before. Augustine kept going. Johnny wanted a smaller place. They could have the farm. It could be perfect. Finally, Augustine relented.

"Will you think about it?"

"Augustine, I always have. But yes, I will."

"Ok."

As the day went on the house transformed, but the real alchemy was happening in the kitchen. Robert and Maggie were allowed back in. Johnny told Robert he would be in charge of making the ice cream, but before he could get started he had to go down to the stream near the old stone springhouse where the water bubbled up year round at the same temperature. There was still some wild watercress near the springhouse. Robert had to go there first and harvest a basketful and on his way back, stop by Johnny's garden. There were still some beets there and Johnny told him exactly where they were. Johnny was going to make as much of the meal as possible with ingredients from the farm. He traded with local farmers for the rest. It would be as fresh a feast as he could prepare. The goose and turkey were freshly killed the day before yesterday. The only thing he prepared in advance was a healthy sized block of goose liver pate carefully wrapped in wax paper, and several jars of chicken stock he planned to use in the mushroom stuffing for the turkey and the apple pork stuffing for the goose.

Johnny knew Maggie had to pick up his sister from New York at the train station, but first she was going to prepare the apples for the four pies. Johnny had collected several varieties of apples, but his secret apples were the wild ones he picked from a gnarly old tree up on the mountain. He took Raphael and had him climb up into the tree where there were still some nice round apples that the deer couldn't reach and the birds hadn't gotten to. Raphael dropped them one by one into a blanket Johnny was holding on the ground like firemen dropping and catching babies from a burning building. These apples had a bite, but they were the essence of apple taste and

Johnny knew how to use them with other apples to leave people wondering what was so special about his pies. He knew that when the sweet, cold ice cream started to melt on the warm, tart pie, it would create a beguiling, simple pleasure that was as American as it could get. For the rest of the meal, he could care less about loyalties to culinary borders. He was of the age where the palate leaned toward France.

When Robert got back, Johnny looked over the bounty.

"Good job," he beamed as he spread the dripping watercress out in his hands like a magician with a deck of cards.

"Ok, are you ready for the hard work? You want to grab yourself a beer?"

"I'm ready."

Maggie was in one corner of the kitchen peeling and slicing the apples. Johnny asked her to carefully keep the varieties separate. He would blend them in the right ratio a little later. Robert could stay in the kitchen over in another corner since he was helping, but also because Johnny wanted to keep an eye on the ice cream process. The ice cream had to be perfect. For the next couple of hours, Johnny filled the aluminum canister with milk and cream, eggs and sugar and just the right amount of vanilla scraped from one bean per batch. The canister was set into a wooden barrel. Robert had to surround it with layers of rock salt and ice and some water and start cranking, turning and turning the metal canister in the super cold bath. Sometimes the churning would be too stiff, the ice seizing around the metal, so then maybe a dash of water, then more ice as it melted, then more salt and churning until the texture was exactly right. Robert was allowed to stay in the kitchen, but what looked like a reward was really Johnny's way of keeping an eye on him. The ice cream had to be perfect. The goose and the turkey were already in the ovens and the smell was beginning to seep through the kitchen. Johnny made the mushroom stuffing for the turkey with golden raisins and morel mushrooms and another stuffing for the goose with apples, onions, garlic and some pork. He was in constant motion, basting this, chopping that. He was making bread, turning vegetables around the goose, quickly closing the oven door not to waste the heat and upset the temperature. With each opening, another waft of aroma would escape like a ghost into the ether of the house. For the most part, the cooking was quiet. There was the short breathing along with the speed stirring of some sauce. There was the hold-your-breath most gentle-fingertip-touch on this or the bold muscular chopping of that. Everything was in service of Johnny's mouth and nose. Again and again, he would feed his own mouth as if it were a little animal, something independent that had ultimate authority. There might be a taste and a pause, a puzzle this time as to what was missing or needed. A taste and a grimace: that would not do, start again or scrap the idea, no negotiating. A taste and barely a reaction: this was where it should be. A taste and a slight smile: a surprise, better than expected, a little gift. Then very rarely, a taste and linger, pause: this time something sublime, something indescribable and the all the work was more than worth it.

By the time Robert had cranked his arms off and the batches, each carefully tasted and spooned out by Johnny into a container in the freezer, had yielded two gallons, the meal was coming together. Robert tried to stay and start helping with cleaning, but Johnny had been methodically cleaning as he went along and really there was only a pile of clean bowls, pots and pans and utensils neatly stacked, leaning on each other on the counter to dry. Johnny finally banished Robert and asked him to check on Augustine and the fires and to make sure all the wood boxes were full near each fireplace.

Augustine began going through the wine cellar, selecting the specific bottles for the evening. As the sun went down, the huge fireplace in the dining room glowed and occasionally popped, the scent of the wood smoke combined with the smells of the cooking which by now had permeated the whole house. All around the house, there were tiny electric candles set in the deep windowsills and on various pieces of antique furniture. Looking into the room was like going back in time a hundred years. In the big library, Augustine had set up sherry near another fireplace that calmly flickered.

The guests would soon be arriving. For the last few years, they were mostly the same. Johnny's sister Florence was a painter. There were several of her big canvases in the house and although her work was usually more abstract, the paintings in the house were pastoral. Florence wasn't that proud of it but she was a very good portrait painter and over the years, she had been commissioned to paint an interesting list of people, from Deans of colleges, to corporate big shots, to English royalty. In the early years, those commissions were her bread and butter. Now she painted what she pleased. Susan, the farm manager, came with her husband Tim, a woodworker, a talented furniture maker. He loved walking around Augustine and Johnny's house, studying the different pieces. He could make things almost that well, but there wasn't much call for pieces that had to be expensive enough to account for the man hours involved. He made much more money building little stools and tables and wine racks and book shelves which were artificially distressed and painted with colonial stencils. He had people take the pieces to farmer's markets all over the state where they were sold next to quilts, vegetables, plastic coolers filled with frozen free range chickens and jars of honey. Bill and Sarah Golden were neighbors. They didn't have any children yet and with each year seemed a little less likely to. Bill had some funny stories. He was the dentist for the New York Bears, a professional hockey team, a job he claimed was professional genius in terms of job security. Hans Redinger was also coming. Hans was in his eighties and he lived alone, but Hans Redinger was not lonely. He lived alone because his wife divorced him when he was seventy-six. She couldn't stand all his girlfriends. Hans was born in Austria. He was Maggies's first serious riding teacher. He had written a couple of books on riding. He was erudite and still handsome. Everyone called him Doctor HR. Robert liked him. He told Robert that when he first came to America, people told him that he needed a title here for people to recognize him as a European expert. He had what amounts to a doctorate in law. He did practice in Austria, although his first love was riding and the camaraderie that was part of it back then. When he came here with his family to escape the psychosis in Austria after the Second World War, he called himself Dr. Redinger. He was certain it helped his horse business immensely. Raphael Hernandez, the farm foreman would be there with his wife Esperanza. There might also be someone from the arts or medicine who happened to be in town for some reason or another.

Maggie returned from the train station with Florence. They all got dressed. As the guests arrived, Johnny offered them drinks. He had sliced small pieces of the warm bread with pieces of the pate. He had outdone himself with the meal and Augustine complemented every course with some of the best burgundy wines from the cellar: clean, crisp white ones for the turkey and delicate, ruby ones as clear as the crystal glasses they sat in for the goose. Robert gave a toast of thanks. He kissed Maggie and thanked her personally for bringing him into contact with all these fine people. Johnny blurted out, "You see Maggie, it's all your fault!" breaking the ice and demanding that everyone eat. They started with the watercress soup. The emerald green soup looked so plain in the white bowls, but every person at one point or another commented on how ridiculously fresh it tasted. Johnny winked at Robert. Then there was the turkey and goose with their stuffings and a butternut squash soufflé. Johnny added only a hint of sugar, letting the natural sweetness of the squash come out by itself. It seemed to allow the taste of the plant to get trapped in the air of the soufflé. The creaminess hid in the bubbles of scent that burst in your mouth. It had to be on the menu every year. There were vegetables that were steeped with flavor from the goose drippings and a healthy dish of quinoa and sunflower seeds that came from the garden. There were roasted beets with fresh goat cheese from the neighbors and tarragon tomatoes sliced in geometric wedges that looked more like a Viennese dessert, a crime to disturb. He kept the last tomatoes of the season going by bringing a few plants into the greenhouse. He wouldn't tell anyone how he still had fresh tomatoes in November. At the end of the meal an empty refrigerator was ready for the leftovers and the dishes were stacked out of sight in the kitchen in a matter of minutes by Robert and Maggie while Johnny and Florence served the warm lattice crusted apple pie with Robert's ice cream. Not a single person passed it up.

Finally, everyone shifted seamlessly into the library for coffee or a sweet, thick Sautern Augustine served so cold you could feel it with your teeth. Robert ended up talking to Hans Redinger. Hans knew Robert was an avid falconer.

"How's the falconry going?"

"Well, I have a very nice bird but unfortunately I haven't been flying her as much as I should. You know how it goes, that job thing."

They both sat down for a little bit near the fire with more wine. They talked about people they both knew but then returned to talking about horses and hawks. Hans opened his suit jacket with a smile. He had a row of cigars in silver canisters lined up in the chest pocket like a bandolier full of bullets. He nodded to Robert, pointing his head toward a door to the porch. In the old days, they would have fired one up right there in the library, but it was different world. They were going to have to sneak outside into the cold. Robert couldn't say no. He thought Hans would lose all respect for him if he did, so they quietly slipped out onto the porch. The sky was clear. Hans handed out the prizes. He lit Robert's and then his own and as he took the first couple puffs, he sighed with a familiar delight. Robert drew the soft smoke and had to fight not to inhale it and hold it in like some fine cannabis. The pleasure was infectious. Hans looked up at the sky.

"My doctor and kids want these out of my life, but Robert, I'll be out here soon. And this won't make a difference."

Robert was going to say something like, you'll be around for quite a while I'm sure, but he realized it would trivialize the moment. He just listened.

"Since I was young, I liked to look out into the night sky. Everywhere I have ever been, I walked out at night and looked up at the same moon and stars and then I would go back home and walk out and look up again and imagine myself instantly back wherever I had been before. I began feeling this connection. We can go somewhere far away, live in a different culture, but there is constancy above, beyond us. I didn't need a religion to give me that comfort."

Robert nodded, he was enjoying Hans's company the same way he liked being around Archie, whether it was their wisdom or a peacefulness that came with their age, it didn't matter. It was very satisfying and somehow fortifying.

"People are always talking about humans and dogs," Hans said, "and humans and cats, but our interests in hawks and horses are some of the oldest relationships between humans and animals."

"It is interesting," Robert answered, "they keep putting the date back as time goes on, but with falconry it goes back five thousand years. What's amazing to me is how popular it became. I read this account of Marco Polo on a month long hunt in the spring of every year with ten thousand falconers led by the great Kublai Khan. Can you imagine that sight?"

"Yes, Robert, and remember everyone was probably on a horse!"

Robert laughed.

"Hans, who do they think were the very first people to use horses?"

"Well, although it coincides with the same timing as falconry and the same place on the steppes of central Asia, it's a little different with horses than falcons because the first people who trained horses used the same horses to capture and eat other horses. They were called the B'Tai. I don't think falconers ever ate their birds, did they?"

Hans looked at Robert, taking another draw on the cigar. The tip grew redder.

"Probably not."

"Horses have had this peculiar relationship with people from the beginning. People used them for travel and domestication and drank their milk for food. They worked them and worshipped them, ate them and drank their blood, all at the same time."

Maggie came out through the door.

"What are you boys doing out here? It's freezing, Robert." She glared at him slightly, her eyes said, the old man doesn't even have a coat on.

They both apologized and snuffed out the cigars. Hans put the ends back in the canisters and slipped Robert's in the hip pocket of

Robert's suit jacket when Maggie couldn't see. They all went back in the house and Maggie stayed with them near the fire as if they needed supervision. She and Hans talked about the old days. She asked him if he was working on any new writing projects. Robert was grateful for her taking over the conversation. He could hardly pay attention, thinking about Sean Nelson and Hans's talk of the B'Tai. The talk in the room quieted down as conversations blended into a relaxed hum. Some deer ran across the driveway as the guest began to leave.

    Robert spent the next day with Maggie, but on Saturday he left for Montana. There he began to read and reread everything Buddhist from back in his days with Archie.

CHAPTER SIX

The Mother Luminosity

Robert did his best thinking while hiking. Even if he were stuck in a city, he would find some route to a park. When he was moving, distractions couldn't catch up with him. Out in the mountains where there was not a house or a person in sight, it seemed easier to think. He was hiking along a windswept ridge. The higher peaks off to the west were already white. To the east was a vast plain. The sky was unusual, with clouds like a vast atmospheric mobile. The breaks in the unending blue sky accented the spaciousness. He felt like a child in a crib, turning under it to see more. It was elemental and strangely comforting to him. He felt smaller, his problems seemed smaller, his decisions less important. Over the years, Robert had come to realize that when he seemed to want to hike more, it meant there was difficulty ahead. He had begun to wonder if he had it all wrong. Maybe there was nothing he was looking for on those wanderings. Maybe he was wandering to avoid what was looking for him. After returning from Thanksgiving, he had been working on another test for Sean. This one was not a medical test. He had finished it. He was going to give it to Sean tomorrow at his next appointment.

When Sean came in, Robert asked him how the work with the heart monitor was going. He said he had been practicing. He thought it was amazing that he could affect his own heart rate himself. Robert encouraged him to keep practicing and said that they would work more on the meditation.

"Sean, I want to try something today. It's kind of a game, if you're ok with that?"

Sean looked at Robert, slightly suspicious. Robert quickly reassured him.

"No, no, it's no big deal. It's kind of like those word association games. I say a word, then the other person says the first word that comes to their mind. For example, if I say hay, the other person might say horse. I say car, the other person says Porsche." They both smiled.

"I'll be honest with you. It usually is nothing, but in this little mental tennis match of thoughts sometimes something will come out, not that the other person is hiding anything. It's just that you kind of trick the brain and something that might be stuck or forgotten breaks loose and just falls out. It can be useful in understanding something that might be under the surface. Does that make sense?"

"Yes." Sean seemed comfortable with Robert's explanation.

"Ok. So what I have done is prepare a series of pictures. They will come up on the computer for a short time. It's not a race, but they will only be up for a few seconds. If you feel you know what the object is or you have seen it before, press one. If you have no idea what it is, press two. I would like you to say yes or no out loud when you press the key, so I will have a backup in case you press the wrong key. Let's try an example."

"Ok," Sean nodded. Robert tapped the keyboard and a picture of a baseball bat came up.

Robert looked at Sean, silently urging him.

"Yes," said Sean as he touched the first key.

"Good." Robert tapped the board again. Sean stared at the picture.

"Fish?" He looked to Robert.

"Well, you can't ask me. They are actually squid. The point is, if you don't know just press two and say no. Do you want to try a couple more?"

"Sure."

They ran through a couple more and Sean got the idea.

"Now, when we start I'm going to leave the room in order to try to limit any influence I may cause even without knowing it, ok?"

"Ok.".

Are you ready? When you're finished, just knock on the door and I'll come back in. Just press start when you're set and it will do the rest."

For the next ten minutes, an array of images came up. For the first few minutes, to set a relaxed rhythm, Robert had arranged clear choices: a chair, a quantum physics equation, hieroglyphics, a fishing pole, a close up of an abstract painting, kittens, the inside of a machine. Then he placed some images he was more interested in. Soon Sean knocked on the door. Robert came in and checked to see if there were any malfunctions and that the recording had worked. He deliberately did not look at any of Sean's answers. They finished the session with more practice on meditating. Later, after Marilyn left the office and Robert was alone, he pulled up Sean's test answers and ran through them. Yes for a fishing pole, no for a high resolution microscopic photograph of cellulose, yes for a snowmobile, no for a die used to make car engine pieces. Robert's pulse was rising. No for a multicellular animal that lived in the deepest ocean trenches beyond any light and then yes for a replica of a lasso made out of hide used by the B'Tai horseman almost seven thousand years ago. Robert sighed. The little hope he had for a different outcome was flickering out. Two more yeses on an ancient unrecognizable saddle and horsehide jacket reconstructed by an archeoanthropologist from fragments of findings that came from the people of the Steppes. He printed the pictures and went home.

He was in the kitchen with Maggie. They were preparing dinner together. There was no better time to bring it up.

"Maggie, you know that patient of mine, Sean?"

"Yes," her back was toward him as she was rinsing vegetables in the sink.

"I think he was reincarnated." His voice was quiet and calm. At first she thought he was joking. She turned around with a cocked smile on her face. She was about to ask what's the joke, but as soon as she saw his face she knew that he was serious.

"What are you talking about? Do you know anything about reincarnation?" There was slight sarcasm in her voice, but before he could answer she caught herself.

"Let me rephrase that. Do you believe in reincarnation?"

"I don't know."

"You don't know? You just made a declaration that you think he was reincarnated, but you don't know if you believe in it. You're not making sense."

"Maggie, I've never experienced a psychiatric breakdown, but I've been able to help many people who have. Jesus, Maggie, last year you and I, who are supposed to be highly trained in science, watched a guy with a stick find a broken water pipe six feet underground. It could have been anywhere in five acres of random ground. We didn't ask any questions when he hit it right on the head, fixed in it a matter of hours, your horses had water again and it saved us thousands of dollars of backhoe work. I don't have to know how everything works in order to help."

"Robert, we're supposed to make professional decisions on the basis of evidence."

He interrupted her quietly. "My problem is the evidence." He went to his briefcase and pulled out the pictures of the lasso and saddle.

"You're a horsewoman. Do you know what these are?"

She glanced at them perfunctorily and pushed them aside. She didn't know. More importantly, she wasn't interested in them at this point.

"Because he does. They're thousands of years old and they're extinct. How does he know what they are? I have a sonogram of sounds he makes that have been analyzed by a top expert to be identical to an eagle, but not just any eagle. A Mongolian eagle. He gets sent to me for a possible psycho-sexual problem stemming from nursing from a horse. We have horses, how did he not get his head kicked off and why a horse when a cow was standing right next to the horse?"

"It's a petting zoo. I told you that. Robert, those animals are there because they are totally safe, precisely because kids might do anything."

"Maggie, the only diagnosis that makes any sense is PTSD."

"So, find the trauma."

"I'm pretty sure I have. He died."

Maggie felt like a well-trained fighter who had been stung by a big blow. She needed a moment to catch her breath, to recover. She needed a clinch. Her temperature was rising, her body was in alarm. She was losing control to threat. She was good at what she did. Her whole life she had trained with some of the best mentalists in the world. She lived with the chess masters. So she slowed down. Her voice changed. To Robert, it was patronizing. She was confident in her skills and certain in her subject. She needed to listen to his case, not to understand what he might be saying, but using his speaking time to formulate what she wanted to say next. She couldn't care about the boy. She had to talk her husband off a ledge.

Robert's practice had become more natural. He was more comfortable with redundant solutions. He was more uncomfortable with singular explanations, suspicious of final outcomes. Sure, every fifteen years or so the great DSM would come out with new criteria to help doctors diagnose mental problems. But to Robert it was a business book. It was for lawyers who needed definitions around criminality and insurance companies who needed definitions to assess blame. In the real world, things got muddy when a borderline personality slipped into a bipolar, which transferred to schizophrenia. He played chess as well, but the people he played with moved the pieces wherever they wanted to.

"Robert, what if this theory were brought up for peer review? What do you think the response would be?"

"Come on, Maggie, peer review?" he said sarcastically. "Your father knew Wayne Jauregg. He injected his patients with malaria to cure syphilitic dementia. His peers thought it was such a good idea that they gave him the Nobel Prize. Do you think it's any different now? People are three to ten times more likely to die from our peers' medical errors than from a car accident. I don't think I have to tell you what a monster our business has become and who our peers are."

Maggie decided it was time to shut things down. Robert continued. He wasn't upset.

"I didn't ask you to believe or not believe, but I wouldn't have minded being able to run a treatment I was thinking about by you."

Maggie had no intentions to hear any thoughts about therapy that would assume she accepted the bizarre premise. They tapered off the conversation. Their meal was uncomfortably silent.

They still had not spoken much by dinner the next night. They were in the kitchen again. Robert wanted to smooth things over. He reached out to touch the small of her back and his hand stopped. She stopped it without seeing. She turned and looked at him. She started in right where they had left off. It hadn't left her mind and she was digging in.

"You told me that his parents are religious. What if they file an ethics complaint? You understand that if you were brought up before a board, I couldn't stand behind you."

"Thanks," he said with a molecule of humor, but there was no room for humor.

"An ethics board," he repeated. "Do you remember when Leave it to Beaver was on television? That's not that long ago. Egas Monig was performing frontal lobotomies. He wasn't pursuing this egoistical destruction on the QT in some sinister state hospital. Where was the ethics board then? Admonished, hell, he's another one who won the Nobel Prize for it, and don't tell me everyone knew the risks. I don't understand. You say you look for the truth, you talk about evidence and logical thinking, but it seems it has to be a certain kind of logic. I would love to know how to do things to get into your particular band of acceptance. It might be nice to go through life with Monig's confidence and certainty, but I think about possible consequences all the time with every patient, with myself every day."

"So do I."

There wasn't going to be a long discussion. Robert had crossed some important line. In a simple sentence, some husband tells his wife he had an affair. In seconds their whole world changes and things can never be the same. But which relationship was the lie: a marriage on autopilot or an affair of reckless passion? Or are both the truth and the lie?

It was a couple of weeks before Christmas. There wasn't any more talk of Sean's therapy. The frigid December air seemed the same inside and outside their house. For Maggie, Robert had slept with another woman.

"Are you going to come to Daddy's for Christmas?" The question was code. Maggie knew the answer, but it was a weak attempt to see if Robert was thinking differently. Had he capitulated? He'd have to come back completely.

"Maggie, we talked about this at Thanksgiving, that I couldn't do both." He sounded apologetic. It was also code. What was he supposed to do? It wasn't like there was any middle ground. She certainly didn't ask him if he would like her to stay with him at Christmas. Was he supposed to deny where his own work was taking him? Shouldn't one of them fight more to keep their relationship alive?

"I know."

"I promised Sam and Jane and the girls I'd go up there for Christmas Eve this year."

There was little more discussion. Maggie left for New York in the middle of the week before Christmas and the day before Christmas Eve she called Robert to say that she was going to stay on another week. She had a couple of meetings with people at the university. They were making serious advances for her to take over the Dean of Psychiatry. She never asked for any input. They were all declarative sentences. For Robert, it had a strong morganatic feel. Robert thought to himself that Augustine still had some clout. In a way he was happy for her, but a familiar sadness was now coming up. All the way up. Things were not going to work out. They were going to break up. It seemed as if he had known this for too long.

CHAPTER SEVEN

The New Year

Robert had talked to Sam, Maggie had talked to Jane and Robert had talked to both Jane and Sam. Maggie wouldn't be back now until just after the New Year. She had accepted the offer in New York. Jane knew the pressure Maggie was under. She agreed to board Maggie's horses at her place. She'd let the girls know more details on an 'as needed' basis. For now, they would know Maggie would be moving to New York and Robert staying in Montana. Maggie was swimming in details, trying to arrange things in Montana and avoid leaving a vacuum while quickly stepping into the big role in New York. Augustine appeared stately on the outside, calmly briefing Maggie on the personalities, where the ghosts were and in what closets as well as being sympathetic to the troubles of her marriage, but on the inside he was ecstatic. She had gotten to the top of the ladder and he still had enough faculties to be part of it. He felt he had been granted two lives on earth.

Robert seemed to be settling after the big, emotional decision. It was now just logistics and time. He knew he had made excuses for their relationship that had seemed too much like a business proposition, but it still hurt. He still loved her, but no amount of rational thinking could budge the discrepancies she created for him. He should have known, he told himself, he married her for reasons. He knew why they matched as a couple. How in the beginning they complimented each other's career. How they had similar taste and liked similar things. They even looked good physically together. It was all so logical. Between psychiatry and horses and hawks they could easily fill their day without any affection. There just wasn't enough time, there were reasons. He knew all the reasons why he married her. What he should have thought more about was that if you know the reason why you want to be around someone or why their voice will capture your hearing even in a crowd or why you will stop walking if you smell they have been in a room, then probably you shouldn't marry them. He felt a ghostlike feeling, a fog catching up, creeping toward him. It was familiar but unsettling. He couldn't pinpoint it.

Christmas Eve was pleasant for Robert at Sam and Jane's. He played the guitar while Carly played the piano and they all sang carols as promised, exchanged gifts and had a beautiful meal. Robert or Maggie had certainly spent time with the Lindleys alone before, either because of conflicting schedules or Maggie's visits to see Augustine, but this time the party was slightly overshadowed by the thought that Maggie's absence might be permanent.

There were no storms in the forecast for the holiday week between Christmas and New Year and no one was going to get any serious business done, so Sam and Robert planned a couple of days to hunt together.

On the next Thursday, they took the birds up to some new country. Sam knew a place where there was sure to be some sharp-tail grouse for Robert to hunt with his peregrine and it was right on the way to the new sage grouse cover Sam had discovered for the gyr falcons.

Robert let Griffin out of his kennel. He was keen. He had been working better and better. His falcon was fit and they had a couple of beautiful flights. Griffin waited like a rock and the hawk streaked in from high. Everything looked professional.

The new sage grouse area was a huge bowl of land miles from mountains off to the west and north and flattening out to the east and south. It was early afternoon but the sun was already dropping by the time Sam decided to fly Nina. When Sam brought her out from her perch in the truck into the sunlight, she looked as if the albedo of the arctic snow was infused in her feathers. She mesmerized Robert. When Sam leaned his face close to hers to catch the hood release in his teeth and deftly slipped it off her head, her giant shimmering black eyes stared at everything so calmly, so confidently, so commandingly that Robert felt he had to step back a little out of respect or because the force of her being pushed him. They both started off on foot and it wasn't long before Sam's dog was getting excited. Sam stopped and freed Nina's leash. She spread her long wings as if to feel the air and when she was ready she pushed off Sam's arm, dropping down a couple feet before the powerful strokes of her wings pulled her quickly up into the sky. She kept up the beats, rising in ever expanding gyres. She was very high and the sky was mostly blue, so it was difficult to see her. Sam sensed trouble. The flights of the other falcons must have gotten the eagles' attention. Sam knew they were around, but he thought they would stay closer to the mountains. Robert could see the concern on Sam's face. Every falconer who hunted seriously up here had lost birds to eagles. If they practiced falconry long enough, falconry practiced on them, but Sam was very careful. He had managed to hunt Miro for a decade and avoid eagles. Maybe Nina stood out even among other birds. Sam screamed up to her. He knew it could help or it could hurt. It might distract the eagle and warn Nina, or it might get Nina's attention and she would miss the incoming eagle. Nina was a large falcon, but the black form hurtling toward her was double her size. As white as she was, the eagle was as dark. Although the eagle might not be as agile as a smaller prey, with its greater mass it could gain incredible speed in freefall stoops. Both birds were dropping fast. It was clear that Nina knew what was heading for her, but she was not maniacally trying to escape. The eagle was gaining on her quickly, using the bright sun as a backdrop of blinding cover. Nina did not seem afraid at all. Perhaps for too long she had been able to overpower anything and she had begun to feel invincible. Both birds passed under a band of white clouds. With the white backing it was easy to see them, the huge, dark eagle rapidly closing in on the falcon. At the last possible moment Nina veered and flipped up, sticking her talons out toward the eagle. It was just enough of a sideways movement to avoid a direct hit, but it was still a bang and the two birds bound together in the sky. Robert glanced at Sam. He was fifty feet away, but Robert could see him flinch as if he himself had been hit and Sam's whole posture drained. Sam was not naïve. He knew both sides of the equation, but this was different. There was no steel in his body. This time something more was at risk. If Robert didn't know for sure before, he knew it then. That bird was bigger than itself. She was Santorina, and Santorina was everything. She was life before three kids and a wife, she was the consequences of only one. She was an incomplete love. She was sex on the soft, thick moss in the endless summer days with no nights. She was the intoxication of immiak and music from a radio. She was the freedom of the arctic, the glacial purity of young thinking. So clear, so natural, so present, she was a falcon and she was a woman. She was nature and she was wildness. She had such a powerful pull because it wasn't fantasy. Sam had been there once – it was real. It was possible. She was still with him after all this time and he never said anything about her. He wanted to be back there. She was a feeling and if Robert hadn't thought she wasn't real then all he needed to do was to look at Sam watching something trying to kill her.

The two birds somersaulted, locked together falling toward the earth and then somehow they broke apart. The eagle rowed its great wings and curved back off towards the mountains. It had made its statement. Sam and Robert expected the gyrfalcon's body to spread out and lifelessly pinwheel toward the earth or, at best, fall in great lopsided arcs, trying to fly with one wing, but she didn't. At least she wasn't dead yet. Sam quickly pulled out a lure to call her in, but he didn't need it. She was coming back toward him on her own. Once he had her in his hands, he was angry with himself. He should have known better.

"How bad is it?"

"I don't know. Can you hold her so I can look?"

"Of course." Robert had never held her before. Her chest was so wide it was difficult to contain her with two hands. She was strong. He had to hold her with considerable strength, not to squeeze her but not to let her move, either. Sam carefully lifted back her feathers. There was some blood and piercings from the eagle's talons. It was impossible to tell how deep they were or if any internal organs were damaged. He carefully extended one wing out and then the other. There was a broken feather and a couple bent ones. Her eyes were clear and she didn't seem shocky. They would have to take her back, treat the wounds and wait, but amazingly she seemed ok.

Jane was waiting in the driveway. Sam had called her. They cleaned all the wounds. They didn't seem that deep and there didn't seem to be any broken bones. Sam started her on some antibiotics, but when he put her on her perch, she seemed ridiculously normal. They would just wait and see.

On his drive home, Robert was thinking about perspectives. A lot depends on which side you are on as the hunter or the hunted, but it is not always easy to know which is which. He wondered if Nina was ok and how she would hunt again. A falcon in the wild can't fear hunting or it would starve, but it might adjust its prey. Would she be more careful because she luckily escaped with her life or would she be emboldened because she held her own with her only threat in the sky? If she was alright, Robert bet that she would hunt exactly the same as she had before. Something else would have to change, like it had for Miro, who hunted differently because he was old.

Nina turned out to be fine. Sam didn't know how that could be, but he decided not to hunt her anymore that year to let her breed and ensure a supply of new birds. Robert hunted with his peregrine and Griffin. They were really jelling as a team.

Right after the New Year, Maggie returned. She only stayed two days. Her time was taken up with meetings at the university. She and Robert thought there was enough going on and that for now they would consider themselves separated and in spring decide on the property and legal matters. It wasn't a good time to sell the house now, anyway. It was easy to fill their conversations with logistics and details so there weren't any emotional silences to pressurize their time together. She would be back in the spring. He'd take care of everything here until then. And that's that, he thought to himself. He didn't want to make things more difficult, but it didn't seem to bother her all that much. Maybe she was just tougher than he was.

Chapter Eight

Wandering in the Bardo

It is best if the guru from whom the deceased received guiding instructions can be had, but if the guru cannot be obtained, then a brother of the Faith; or if the latter is also unobtainable, then a learned man of the same Faith; or should all these be unobtainable, then a person who can read correctly and distinctly ought to read this many times over. Thereby [the deceased] will be put in mind of what he had [previously] heard of the setting-face-to-face and will at once come to recognize that Fundamental Light and undoubtedly obtain liberation.
—The Tibetan Book of the Dead

After the holidays, winter had settled in. To a certain extent, Robert welcomed the routine. It seemed easier to concentrate being alone. He seemed a little melancholic, but it wasn't all a bad feeling. There was a subtle relief from the relentless questioning pressure he had always felt in his relationship with Maggie. That was gone, but it left a hole and a vacuum was a vacuum. He was anxious to begin Sean's treatment. He asked James and Patricia Nelson to come in for a meeting. Now, the great Liberation Through Hearing, the Bardo Thodol. The Tibetan Book of the Dead would be the template to help Sean in the next few weeks. Robert had practically memorized the recitations and protocol that were about to begin. As he waited for the Nelson's to arrive, he watched a sound experiment that someone had sent him on his computer. Salt from a simple shaker was poured like snow on to a dark, flat metal square that would vibrate with the sound of a tone. A low tone sounded at three hundred forty five Hertz. As if by magic, the crystals of salt like white ants seemed to come alive and line up as to the choreography of some complex marching band. Another tone sounded at one thousand Hertz. A kaleidoscope click of patterns as the white salt realigned on the dark plate into repeating rounded squares. Another tone higher, another realignment and the lines became like striated bands of muscle fibers identically repeating. Another higher tone and now a block of hieroglyphics matching as if each were carefully painted. With each higher tone, more complex patterns like snowflakes reformed, a new tone now near the upper range of the human register instantly produced the pattern of an intricate Amish quilt. How, he thought to himself. It was beautiful and almost frightening.

He glanced at his guitar. He remembered his mother asking his father to play. She went somewhere with the sound. He never knew where. We don't know anything about anything, he thought to himself. He was buckling himself up for a ride. If Maggie's, reaction to his thoughts about Sean was any indication, he knew he would have to be careful. The intercom buzzed. The Nelson's had arrived. Robert got up and opened the door to the waiting room.

"Thank you both for coming in. Please come in and sit down."

When everyone was settled, Robert started.

"I have an idea of treatment I'd like to try with Sean. I have gone over his history and symptoms carefully. I don't feel he's autistic or bipolar. In cases like these, we don't really have a choice but to use medications. We try different types and dosages, but the severity of the condition usually requires them. We don't know the long-term effects of the SSRI's and we all know Sean doesn't like the side effects. As you are well aware, the terminology is always changing, but what I feel he suffers from is Post Traumatic Stress Disorder."

James winced and seemed slightly defensive.

Robert looked at him. "James?" James was all too familiar with the plague of PTSD in the military.

"But Doc, he hasn't had any trauma."

Robert spoke carefully. "That is difficult to say. Maybe on some level we may not even know about yet, he has. Take two people who have an equal fear of heights. One has no biographical history of any experience that might cause the reaction, whereas another person we know fell out of a building when they were very young. If we treat them both the same, they often respond the same. I don't feel we need to know the exact cause, because after the fact the brain can respond similarly. A veteran from Iraq with PTSD and a police officer with PTSD might both benefit from the same kind of treatment even though their precipitatory causes might be very different.

Robert began explaining the treatment. He could hear himself on script. The irony of calmly talking about extinction learning when all his effort was going toward learning about extinction did not escape him. He was actually feeling slightly disingenuous with his explanation. On the other hand, he already knew how far he would get talking to Christians in Montana about freeing someone stuck in the Bardo.

"The problem is, what if we can't uncover some events or a series of events that are the cause, or what if the cause is something we don't understand yet, maybe a genetic mutation, anything. If we can't uncover a familiar cause, does this nullify the possible benefits of the treatments? Does this mean the person is doomed to their paralyzing fears? Am I making any sense?"

They both answered, "Yes." James seemed a little reassured.

"My aim is to taper off the drugs through using our therapy sessions and incorporate the cognitive behavior therapy. And I'm not talking about years here, what I have in mind is a seven week period. I'm not saying that there won't have to be work after that, but I think it will be relatively dramatic. We can have the benzodiazepine on hand on an as-needed basis, but I want to really try not to use it. I'd give you a specific dosage drop of the other meds per week. You have my phone numbers. If he is struggling, call me, twenty-four hours a day. I have a special short range phone that I would like him to have for the next few weeks. It won't work long distance, so that isn't a problem. Would you be open to letting him have it, so he could feel he can reach me anytime, if he feels it is serious? You can think about that and let me know at our next session. As you know, he has been using the heart rate monitor and I have been impressed with his response to working with it and understanding it. I'm going to try to dig a little deeper to uncover the mechanics of these fears more so than the cause. We can't change the past – it's going to be about moving forward. I'd like to begin at our next session. Is that ok?"

They both nodded their approval.

"There's one more thing. As part of my job, you know I try to stay neutral on political and religious issues, topics that might alienate someone who needs my help. But I know you are a religious family and we don't have to go any deeper than that, but if you feel like saying a prayer for him, especially next week, I think it could help."

James nodded reverently. Patricia said she prayed for him all the time. Robert smiled. A true mother, he thought. Neither seemed to wonder why he would ask them to do this.

"I'll keep you posted and I'll see all of you with Sean next Thursday."

After they left, Robert went to the lavatory. He looked at himself in the mirror. "I hope you know what you are doing," he thought out loud.

CHAPTER NINE

In the Bardo

Alas! While wandering alone, separated from living friends,
When the vacuous, reflected boy of mine own mental ideas dawneth upon me,
May the Buddhas, vouchsafing their power of compassion,
Grant that there shall be no fear, awe, or terror in the Bardo.
—The Tibetan Book of the Dead

"Sean, I want to begin today a kind of new treatment for the next few weeks. I'd like to see if we can cut back or even eliminate the meds you're on, but this is going to be coupled with some serious training for you and I. Your parents have my number and they agreed to let me give you this phone. It's limited range, but you will be able to reach me if you feel you need to, at any time."

Sean liked the phone. Robert saw him looking it over.

"Remember, it's not a toy."

Sean smiled.

"I'd like to start with the dream or nightmare, whatever we want to call it, about the nothingness. Especially if a person dies, the complete void, the way you told me how frightening that is, just the thought of the end of the world."

Sean was now alert. He was a little anxious about the new therapy and now Robert seemed to be purposely guiding him toward those thoughts that he could barely talk about. He was quickly becoming uncomfortable, but then it seemed Robert changed the subject.

"You like camping, right?"

"Yes." He felt a little annoyed, like he was being manipulated. He thought Robert knew that he liked camping.

"Ok, let's say a group of friends go camping. We have this nice hike up into the mountains, maybe some fishing or we take the kayaks out on the lake, but its late afternoon, so we pitch our tents and then as it gets dark we build a fire. We talk and cook something delicious on the fire. Later, we get in our sleeping bags. We can still feel a little of the heat and see the glow of the crackling embers. We have a great night's sleep. In the morning, we look at the fire pit and it's out cold, the big pile of wood is gone. The wood has disappeared."

Robert looked at Sean, checking to see if he was with him. He was listening intently.

"Or has it disappeared?"

Sean looked at him. He wasn't sure what to say.

"What I am suggesting is that things can change. The wood burned as fuel for the fire, we cooked our food with it, it also helped keep us warm. It is even beautiful just to stare at and it gave us light to see back to our tents in the dark. It also produced smoke and gas and obviously if a person were to breathe that in, they could die. In the morning, there are only ashes. The heat may have risen into the atmosphere with the smoke. In the world that we live in, including space, things are changing all the time. A solid piece of wood turns into heat and gas and light. A different gas might condense, turning into liquid like clouds to rain. Stars burn out over a really long time like fires and turn into bodies with gravitational fields. The more we seem to understand about the universe, the more the idea that the energy of something could completely disappear seems impossible. Things seem to be in a constant flow, some faster, some slower but always changing, rearranging. That flow is natural. When things don't flow there is a problem and when people try to stop that flow, there are problems. When you have that frightening dream, it's almost as if the universe is stuck. We could find a hundred proofs to show you the universe is not stuck, that it has not stopped, but when you are in the middle of that I don't think you will believe anyone who says so. I think your dream is like a painting. It looks like something but has underlying meaning. I think that at least partially it means you are stuck. All this emptiness, aloneness – it's not right. We have to try to get it unstuck. Does what I'm saying make any sense?"

"Yes." It did make sense. But he wondered how this was going to make him feel better.

"Let's say a person is in the middle of New York City, and this person is so afraid of getting lost that they start to panic and they start running back to where they thought they started from. They run back to the last place they turned, then the next turn, then they think, no, this is not right, they start running faster, they're in a mess. They dart right across a street and get hit by a car and are killed. What killed them, the car or panic? Being lost can be a state of mind, hysteria can be disastrous."

Sean interrupted. "But being lost can be a disaster."

"That's true. Do you feel lost?"

"Not now. But I feel like it could happen."

"I think it would be normal for a person to get very anxious if they were lost. What bothers me is if they are anxious when they are not lost or if their anxiety is preventing them from finding their way out. Or, like the person in New York, it may even cause them harm. Maybe now we won't be able to find the cause of your anxiety, but I think we can find a way to control it. Are you still using the heart rate monitor?"

"Yes. Sometimes my heart rate goes down when I just put it on. I don't even have to start thinking about it."

"That's amazing, isn't it? Now I have something more I want you to try." Robert had a saddle on a sturdy wooden stand that was curved round like the back of a horse.

"You like to ride horses, don't you?"

"It's ok." He didn't tell Robert that he didn't like horses. He wasn't afraid of them. He just didn't really like them.

"Ok, I'd like you to get up on the saddle."

Sean climbed up.

"Now, sit up straight, your stomach in, your core strong, make sure you keep your shoulders back and down. You must keep really good posture, but not too tense. You can hold your hands together. Think of holding reins."

As Robert adjusted his position, he could hear Maggie in his head, talking about how kids seemed to naturally have good position on a horse, but the more lessons they take the more contorted they become as instructors start molding them into different styles. The point was good riding position was the same as the position for meditation or the martial arts. Robert could see that Sean was beautifully balanced with just a few corrections.

"Now," Robert said, "I want you to imagine that you are a great general, you are riding through a battle, you seem to be able to ride slowly right through the chaos, your troops are fighting, getting wounded, dying. Occasionally in all the horror, sometimes for a moment you see that the countryside is beautiful, but your attention comes back to the sounds and smells of the awful war. This feeling of the way you stay sitting on your horse, this powerful, steady horse is going to be important. Things might be coming by you, for you. Things you can't control. Stay in the saddle and keep track of your heart rate and breathing. As things come and go, don't get stuck, everything will change. We're going to practice this until it works in a real situation. You know I have always tried to level with you, right?"

Sean nodded.

"No, I need a verbal answer."

"Yes."

"This position is serious. It's not a game, you get that, right?"

"Yes."

"You see this position is actually very common. You see it in sports training, in dance training, in martial arts. In the beginning of karate, one of the first stances they teach you is the horse stance, but that is a mistake in translation. A horse stance would be on all fours." Robert jumped down and showed him. "Did your Dad ever give you horse rides on his back like this when you were little?"

Sean smiled yes.

Then Robert stood up, flexed his knees and rooted himself to the floor with a straight upper body.

"This is the horse stance, but it should have been called the rider's stance because you see it is the same as your position on that saddle. This position is almost magical, it is grounding, very physically secure, strong and balanced. It is the same position used in meditation. I want you to practice this every day for a few minutes. Things might come into your awareness – let them go. Simple things like having to go to the bathroom all of a sudden. The better you get at it, the better you will be able to control bigger distractions, anxiety, hallucinations. The peaceful images will come from your heart. I think you can see that already from your work with the heart monitor. The frightening images will come from your brain. As we reduce the medications, they may come back. You will let them pass. Like the general on the horse, you must go through the awfulness. It will change and pass by unless you stop it by grabbing on to it. You have my phone if you need me. You may find you become more sensitive to sounds than is normal. Try to sleep on your right side. If the dreams come, look for a light. I don't know how it might appear, but if you see anything like this let me know, especially a blue light."

Sean was a little nervous. Robert asked him to get down off of the saddle and try the position on the floor. Sean knelt down and rested on his heels.

"Perfect."

"I don't want to alarm you, but I want to be prepared. We're going to fix this."

Sean nodded.

They spent the rest of the session with small talk and Robert reminded him before he left to practice.

By the time Robert got home from the office it was dark. He

took Griffin out for a run in the snow. It was getting dark so early now. In late January, winter was locking in. The air was antiseptic, no bugs. It was mountaineer's air for the whole population. The white dog galloped in the dry snow, leaving plumes of the powder to settle back down to the earth. Robert recited the prayer for the transfer of consciousness seven times, the steam of his breath rose into the clear atmosphere. He recited them whenever he could. He read them for the boy he never knew. He read them for the emerging Sean. He read them for Maggie. He read them for himself. He read them for help from any and all the falcon angels.

Chapter Ten

The Second Week

If at this stage, one does not meet with this kind of teaching, one's hearing [of religious lore] – although it be like an ocean [in its vastness] – is of no avail. There are even discipline-holding abbots [or bihkkhus] and doctors in metaphysical discourses who err at this stage, and, not recognizing, wander into the Sangsara.
—The Tibetan Book of the Dead

The night before his next session with Sean, Robert's phone rang at three o'clock in the morning. He was waiting for it, but it wasn't Sean. It was Maggie. He had not heard from her in a couple weeks. Her voice was quaking. She wasn't crying, but was close to it.

"Hey, what's wrong?"

He was waking up fast. She didn't know what was wrong, she said, she just felt upset, nervous. It was hard for him to listen. He couldn't stop himself from feeling a little excited that she'd called him. Was this some opening gambit toward reconciliation? It was the same way he couldn't stop his heart from going out to some child that needed something. There wasn't much control, it was his mother's genes. He knew he had to slow down and stop reading things into two short sentences of conversation. They talked for a little while. She was crying a little. It wasn't like her. He tried to be comforting, nothing deep. She was probably understandably a bit overwhelmed by the stress. She seemed to settle down and then almost abruptly wanted to end the conversation. He didn't try to hang on. He didn't sleep well the rest of the night.

In the morning he felt he needed to check back with her, but he decided to wait until around noon so he wouldn't seem pressing. He called her from his office. She seemed like a very different person. She sounded almost ashamed that she had called him. She didn't want to talk anymore and was short with him. He politely backed up or was backed up and ended the call. There was no room for him to talk. Afterwards, he felt stung. He would be a little bit more careful if it happened again. Whatever it was, it was no opening gambit. Then he caught himself. What would he have done if it was? He hadn't even thought about those consequences. Would he go back? What if she completely turned around – was it fixable? What would he say to her? What would have to change?

Patricia Nelson dropped of Sean at Robert's office. Robert spoke with her briefly, everything seemed to be going ok, she was going to continue on some errands and come back to get him.

"So," Robert asked Sean, "How did the week go?"

"Fine."

"Practicing the sitting?"

"Yes."

"Good, any bad dreams?"

"Not too bad."

"I was thinking about something from our last meeting that I wanted to try to go over. Is that ok?"

"Sure."

"Well, you know when I was talking about the general on his horse, how he was seeing awful destruction and then maybe a moment of peaceful beauty, but the horse kept walking? I didn't mean you would want to live a life where nothing reaches you. Suppose there's a kid who wanted to play football but is afraid of getting hurt. It's easy, don't play and you will never get hurt, but you will also never feel the exhilaration of charging downfield with your teammates or making some great touchdown. Life is about participation. Life is to be experienced. You can't always choose good or bad experiences. Some parts of life, you have very little control. When I was talking about the general, I was talking about the part where we can have some control."

"I don't like when things get out of control. I think it's worse not to control your mind."

"Worse than what?"

"Worse than getting hurt."

"You mean physically hurt like a football injury? The mental pain is worse than the physical part?"

"Yes."

"I get that," Robert said. "Sean, let's say you're planning something and a snowstorm cancels the event. That is something we pretty much cannot control. You're not talking about that kind of control, are you?"

"No, it's when my brain gets swirling and I can't stop it."

"I understand, Sean, but the more we study the brain the more we see that people will argue that they make or made this decision or that in total control. Yet, we know if we play a certain kind of music at a car dealership people will buy a blue care when they came in for a red one. There are things that will trick the brain. Besides that, our brains want to have things settled, organized, compartmentalized quickly and it doesn't always care if the story it makes up is true. People who always seem to see things clearly and always have an answer may be deceiving themselves, whereas the person who is not so certain and holds off can end up closer to the truth. All I'm saying is control is a complicated subject. A balanced person is not going to be necessarily in control or feel they are in control all the time. Some things in life will be unsettling, conflicting. Don't be afraid of unsettling feelings. Let them out. Don't try to bury them or constantly push them away or answer them immediately. They won't get addressed or corrected that way. They just fester, they aren't gone. They are just covered over. And they take a toll, you see?"

Sean nodded yes.

"I've always leveled with you. There are some cases of psychological problems, a brain malfunctions that must be medicated, the problem is so severe it has to be calmed down for the person to function, but I don't think this is your case. I think we can fix what is bothering you. I'm not saying it will be easy, but I feel it is a different problem."

Sean nodded again.

"Ok, I want to practice the sitting and breathing, but I also want to talk a little more about your dreams or visions aside from the meditation. When they come, don't let them control you. We have to keep practicing not to get pulled in by them. One of the things you must watch for in the middle of them, when you get in that place, is whether there is any light. I can't help you as to what it might look like, but think of it as a positive thing. It will not be harmful, so we need to try to find it."

They practiced together. Robert tried to get Sean to describe the terrors. All the while he made sure Sean knew he had a lifeline, it was just practice in his office. All their small talk about sports and school was beginning to pay off. They were polishing the wires of communication. Sean had to talk. It was all Robert had to guide him.

Two nights later, the phone finally rang. Patricia called, she said Sean was pretty upset and wanted to call him. Robert told her he was glad to know Sean would call.

"Can he talk to me in private?"

"Yes."

"Ok, Patricia, let's see how this goes. I don't want to give him any meds. If he doesn't calm down, give him the placebo. If he is still distressed by morning, call me. I'll have Marilyn fit him in sometime tomorrow. Hopefully he'll be alright and we can keep to his regular appointment next week."

"Good." She spoke quickly; she wanted to give the phone back to Sean.

"Sean, what's going on?"

Sean took the phone and went to his room.

"I had a really bad dream. I can't close my eyes."

"Did you try the breathing?"

"Yes. It's too strong."

"Ok, don't worry about that for now. Can you tell me about the dreams?"

"I was in a strange place. It felt like where we live, but everything was different, nothing was right. I was floating above myself."

"There were two of you?"

"Yes, the one on the ground was a corpse. It was being torn apart by beings, they were eating me. I'm dead, Dr. Rob. I see myself being dead." He was crying.

"Sean, how can you be dead if you are the one watching? The other boy is dead."

"I am the other boy."

"Not anymore. You can't be. You are talking to me. I know it is terrible, but you need to ground yourself. You must let those visions pass. This is what we have been practicing. I told you they would come. Look around the room. You are here now and your mother is in the next room. Let's try to breathe. Are you sitting in the position?"

"Yes," he struggled to get there, but the sound of Robert's voice was working.

"Sean, where is the heart rate monitor?"

"It's right here on my table," his voice was uneven, cracking.

"Can you put it on?"

"I think so."

"Tell me when it's on."

"It's on."

"What does it read?"

"One hundred forty." It was high enough for a strong athletic activity.

"Ok, let's bring it down. Sean, I am convinced something awful happened, but I don't know what it was. But whatever happened is over. We need to go on."

"It feels very, very sad."

"I know, I know. In the dream, did you see any lights?"

"I can't remember. It was so real. It was daytime."

"Ok." In the background Robert could hear the beep of the monitor dropping. They talked more and finally the heart rate was near normal. Robert asked him if he thought he could rest. He didn't have to close his eyes, he just needed to let things pass by and keep the phone near him. If he needed to they could meet tomorrow, if not he would see him in a few days. Robert asked him if he could hang up. Sean said ok. In a little while, Patricia checked on Sean. He was asleep. She shut the phone off. At home, Robert was reciting the prayers until he fell asleep.

CHAPTER ELEVEN

The Third Week

[Instructions to the Officiant]: Again, if through great weakness in devotions and lack of familiarity one be not able to understand, illusion may overcome one, and one will wander to the doors of wombs. The instruction for the closing of the womb-doors becometh very important; call the deceased by name and say this: O nobly-born, if thou hast not understood the above at this moment, through the influence of karma, thou wilt have the impression that thou art either ascending, or moving along a level, or going downwards. Thereupon, meditate upon the Compassionate One. Remember. Then, as said above, gusts of wind, and icy blasts, hail-storms, and darkness, and impression of fleeing into places of misery; those who are endowed with meritorious karma will have the impression of arriving in places of happiness. Thereupon, O nobly-born, in whatever continent or place thou are to be born, the signs of that birthplace will shine upon thee then.
—The Tibetan Book of the Dead

For a few years now to break up the long winter, Jane and Sam took the girls on vacation in South America. The falconry season was over for all intents and purposes, the girls had a break in school and if they took a couple extra days the whole family could have almost ten days in the warmth and sun. Sam had an old friend, Bernardo Legoretto, whom he had met on a falconry project.

Bernardo was a wealthy man and he loved hosting the Lindley's at a place he had on the ocean. It was a private place. One of the reasons he bought it was to secure it so the Agriculture and Wildlife Ministry could band and study the migrating falcons that came on the flyways all along the Atlantic coast from North America. Bernardo got to talk falcons with Sam and show him his birds and breeding program and the ladies enjoyed the sun and beach. Sam asked Robert if he would take care of the birds while they were away. Robert had stopped by one evening before they left so that Sam could fill him in on what had to be done. Sam went over everything with him. They walked into the house where Sam showed him the freezer with falcon meals. Jane gave Robert a hug and insisted he stay for an early dinner. She reminded him he didn't have to worry about the house or the dogs and cats or horses. A friend of hers that Robert had never met would be house sitting. She drove a green jeep, so if he saw that car up here he would know who it was. The girls were in and out through the meal. Everyone had to work or go to school the next day.

As Robert drove home, it was bleak. The sky was overcast. They were calling for snow so there weren't even any stars out. Robert's mind was on Sean. Their appointment was tomorrow. He was anxious to see him after the phone call.

Robert spoke briefly with Patricia Nelson before his session with Sean. She had not given him any medication the night of the call. He had fallen asleep. He seemed exhausted the next day, but ok. They had continued the taper of his normal meds and were now almost down to nothing.

"Hello, Sean."

"Hi, Dr. Rob."

"How's school?"

"Ok."

"So, you had a bit of a rough night a couple days ago?"

"Yes." Sean spoke quietly.

"The important thing is that we got through it. It's like our practice. The more we do, the better we get."

They talked for a while and then Robert asked Sean, "Why did you think the body being torn apart was you?"

"Because it was me."

"Ok, but somehow you were looking down at it. You were out of that body and you are here now."

"Did I go to heaven?"

"That's a good question. I have not heard of anyone coming back from heaven, so I don't think so, but people have come back from being clinically dead. There is a medical field now that specializes in resuscitation. People who have had a heart attack and had their brain become inactive would be considered dead. But some people have been revived as long as a half an hour or more after dying. Sometimes when they come back, they say things that would suggest that even though they were clinically dead, there was some consciousness. They say they knew what was going on in the hospital room and they heard the doctors talking. Doctors are trying to test this. We don't know enough yet. Sometimes it seems like you get stuck in a place like that but I don't think that place is heaven. I don't know if it's real, but what does it matter? If you are stuck, you're stuck. I want to try to move forward."

Sean nodded his head in agreement.

"Sean, everyone has to die. I don't want to focus on that. I want to focus on now, on life and all the amazing things that can happen and how we are going to get there. You have to understand. I am not telling you to think some happy Disneyland thought to make it all better. We have been working hard. I think we're close. It's a matter of training the brain."

Sean smiled. He liked the rhyme.

"Train my brain."

"Yes, we'll do it. Keep practicing with the monitor. If the dark things come up again, try your best to hear me. You will need to look for any light, and if you see it focus on it. Think of it as the light of God, if you want."

Robert was feeling good about Sean. In general, Sean was making better decisions and his schoolwork was improving. He was listening to Robert but there was another part. This deeper part hadn't shifted; it was in a different frame of time.

Robert left the office a little early. Jane and Sam and the girls had left for their trip over the weekend. Robert was on his way up to their place to feed and check the birds again. It was snowing lightly but the wind was so strong that when he got out of his truck it felt like a blizzard. He had to remember to get more food out of the freezer in the house when he finished, to thaw out for tomorrow. The birds were all fine. Secure in the hawk house, they seemed oblivious to the weather, resting like cats. He walked over to the main house with his head cocked, protecting his face from the abrasive snow. The lights were on and the green jeep was parked in front. He opened the door into the kitchen quickly and stepped in, stomping the snow off of his feet on the door rug and shaking the snow out of his hair. When he looked up, she was standing by the stove completely naked.

"God! I'm so sorry!" he blurted out, but he wasn't sorry at all. She was stunning. Her body was fit and strong, rounded a little like a swimmer. She had thick black hair divided by her shoulders.

"No, no," she stopped him. "It's not your fault. I knew you were out there. I just wanted to check the temperature on the stove before I went into the shower." She finished her sentence calmly, as if she were completely dressed. There was no embarrassed covering up. She just said, "Please excuse me for a second," and she walked out of the kitchen.

Jesus, thought Robert as she walked into the other room, she's even better from behind. She came back in a moment with a robe on. She walked toward Robert to shake his hand. He hadn't even realized he had not moved an inch from the small rug by the door. He stood waiting like a well-trained puppy.

"I'm Cypress Ferrin. I'm sorry if I offended you."

Robert shook her hand, they were about the same height and Robert noticed her blue eyes.

"Robert McPherson. I think that it was the opposite of being offended."

She smiled at the compliment.

"What was your first name?" he seemed to recall Jane telling him about a house sitter, but she clearly didn't elaborate.

"Cypress. My parents named me after a tree." She raised her eyebrows with a half-smile.

"But everyone calls me Ressa."

"Oh, that's a beautiful name. Actually, both of them."

She laughed lightly. "Thanks."

"I just have to get some chicken out of the freezer for the birds. Is that ok?" He finally stepped off the rug.

"Of course." She stepped back to clear the way. He wanted to find some excuse to talk more, but he felt it was already an awkward enough first meeting, so he brought out the meat, apologized again for interrupting her space and stepped back out into the wind which didn't seem nearly as cold. As he drove back home to take care of his own animals, he couldn't get the image of her out of his mind. The black Irish, he thought, that dichotomy between the dark, rich hair and the bluest of eyes. And that body.

CHAPTER TWELVE

The Fourth Week

In that state wherein thou art existing, there is being experienced by thee in an unbearable intensity, voidness and Brightness inseparable – the Voidness bright by nature and the Brightness by nature void, and the Brightness inseparable from the Voidness – a state of the primordial [or unmodified] intellect, which is the Adi-Kaya. And the power of this, shining unobstructedly, will radiate everywhere; it is the Nirmana-Kaya.
—The Tibetan Book of the Dead

The night before their next session, Robert got another phone call from Sean. This time, he seemed to still be half inside the dream state. He was agitated and scared.

"What's going on?"

"I'm in that bad dream I told you about."

"Which one? Can you tell me more?"

"The one where everything is gone, the blackness. I was being blown into the universe, into blackness. It was getting darker and colder. The wind was stronger and stronger. I couldn't hold on much longer. The planets were getting farther and farther away. I could hear voices, but I couldn't tell what they were saying. Everything was spreading out." Sean was sniffling and fighting back his anxiety.

"Dr. Rob, I can't get back to everyone. I'm being pulled away to the blackness."

"Sean," Robert tried to get his attention.

"Yes?"

"You got back, that's part of the problem. Are the stars light and shiny like the stars I can see at night out my window now?"

"Yes, like that but getting even farther away."

"Sean, go back there. You are going the wrong way. You're fighting like a fish in a powerful stream. You're getting exhausted, fighting all the time against the unstoppable current. Turn around and let go. Follow the light. Let the wind take you. You have to see where it goes. You have to try. Where you are is no good, you can't hold on there. You'll be ok. I'm certain of it. This time, let's do it differently. Start your breathing and let yourself go and put your energy into following the light. Don't let fear stop you. Break through this time."

"I don't know," he mumbled weakly.

"Maybe it won't come back, but if it does you have to try. We'll be having a session tomorrow. I will want to hear what happened. Will you try? I'm going to pray with you. Trust me."

"I'll see," he was steadier, calmer, listening to Robert's voice.

"Remember, I'm here. You are not alone. You will be able to reach me, ok?"

They talked for a little while longer. Their voices trailed off and the phones clicked off. Robert waited for it to ring back. He started reciting.

> *Alas when he is wandering in the Sangsara, through force of overpowering illusions,*
> *On the light-path of the abandonment of fright, fear and awe,*
> *May the bands of the Bhagavans, the Peaceful and Wrathful Ones, lead him,*
> *May the bands of the Wrathful Goddess Rich in Space be his rearguard,*
> *And save him from the fearful Ambuscades of the Bardo,*

> *And place him in the state of the Perfectly-Enlightened Buddhas*
> *When wandering alone, separated from dear friends,*
> *When the void forms of one's own thoughts are shining here,*
> *May the Buddhas, exerting the force of their grace,*
> *Cause not to come the fear, awe, and terror of the Bardo.*
> *When the five bright Wisdom-Lights are shining here,*
> *May recognition come without dread and without awe;*
> *When the divine bodies of the Peaceful and the Wrathful are shining here;*
> *May the assurance of fearlessness be obtained and the Bardo be recognized.*
> *When, by the power of evil karma, misery is tasted,*
> *May the tutelary dieties dissipate the misery;*
> *When the natural sound of Reality is reverberating like a thousand thunders,*
> *May they be transmuted into the sounds of the Six Syllables.*
> *When unprotected, karma having to be followed here,*
> *I beseech the Gracious Compassionate One to protect him;*
> *When suffering miseries of karmic propensities here,*
> *May the blissfulness of the Clear Light dawn;*
> *May the Five Elements not rise up as enemies;*
> *But may he behold the realms of the Five Orders of the Enlightened Ones.*

Robert recited the prayer two more times. He slept fitfully and then worked through the next day, but his attention was on his upcoming session with Sean. When he came in the office, Robert saw that Sean looked different. He didn't seem slouched over. He looked brighter. They sat down. This time, there wasn't any small talk.

"What happened? You didn't call me back."

"What were you singing?" Sean had turned the tables. Robert just looked at him.

"I heard your voice and your guitar."

"My guitar." Robert was incredulous. "I've never played my guitar for you."

"I heard it. The dream came right back. I turned around in this strong wind to hear you and I slipped. I was falling into space. But the sound was in front of me so I let go. I wasn't afraid."

"What happened then?"

"I thought you brought the light you've always asked about because I caught up with the stars that were flying away. In a few seconds, I got close. I wasn't cold. It got warmer and warmer and brighter."

"Did it hurt your eyes?"

"I wasn't paying attention with my eyes. I was listening, hearing. The sound could go right through the blackness. The blackness wasn't the end. The song could go right through it. I wasn't afraid anymore. It didn't matter, light or dark. It was the sound, the feeling. Not what I was seeing."

"Amazing. Then what happened?"

"Then I was back in my bed. I was ok and really tired. I fell asleep but I don't know how."

Now it was Robert's pulse that was racing. He tried to calm down and find some rational language.

"Sean, I think that what you did was very brave and very important. You conquered that fear. I'm not saying it will be the last of it, but things will not be the same. Now you know you have done it, it can be done. You are not trapped by all the walls of protection that don't really protect you. We all need to live like you just did, to look into the eyes of fear and let it go. We don't have to be slaves to those hellish games the mind can play. We can let them go and direct our attention to positive actions. Your fears have tried to keep the demons away, they convinced you they would protect you, but you became their prisoner. This time you didn't listen to them. You didn't try to hide. When there were no people you weren't even afraid of being alone. Isn't that interesting? All by yourself like some astronaut you traveled the cosmos and you didn't get lost. This is a new you. We need to build on this. The loneliness will be gone. We have to keep practicing so this will not be so difficult. We have to encourage this new you. I know we're both going to like him. I'm not saying it will be easy. I just think all the effort will feel like it's paying off. Now let's keep down these walls of protection, which you have seen don't work, and look for more new connections."

Sean listened intently but the talking was not that necessary. He knew what Robert was trying to say. Deep inside he felt it. He just knew it. Words were almost a waste of time. He knew something had changed.

Robert felt excited about their session. He wondered where it would go now. He knew if he were a monk in Tibet it would be complete in around two weeks.

That evening, Robert drove out to feed Sam's birds. He had been anticipating seeing her each time he drove in, but after the first dramatic meeting, Ressa's jeep had not been there and now there were only a few days before Sam and Jane would return. As he drove down the road before the turn into Sam and Jane's drive, he felt a little embarrassed with himself. She was too young for him. She was certainly in some relationship. Still, he couldn't stop his pulse from quickening when he saw her jeep parked near the house. He took care of the birds, went back to his truck to look at himself in the mirror and then went up to the house and knocked. Finally, she came to the door.

"Hi Robert, you didn't have to knock."

"Hi." He walked in and he looked at her, at her clothing, probably for too long.

"Disappointed?" she teased.

Robert McPherson was not usually ever at a loss for words and even now he didn't feel he didn't know what to say, it was just that his eyes were transfixed. They didn't want to let go, as if they were trying to memorize her in case she disappeared.

"No," he finally spoke, "Frankly, I was disappointed the last couple days. You weren't here when I came up and I thought to myself, that's it, the first and last time I'll see her."

"I teach a class a few evenings a week at the university."

"What do you teach?"

"Chemistry. It's just part time. I do it for a little extra money in the winter. Mainly I'm a conservator. I'm doing some work for the same firm as Sam."

"Oh. That's how you know them?"

"Yes. I'm from the Seattle area. I haven't been here long, but they have been very nice to me. Jane and I work out at the same gym."

Robert looked at her hands. There wasn't any wedding ring. He'd have to explain his. She had a glass of wine on the counter and was obviously going to prepare some dinner.

"Would you like a glass of wine?"

"Yes, I would love one, let me just get the bird meals ready for tomorrow. Have you met Sam's falcons?"

"Yes, they are exquisite animals. They took me hunting once. The collaboration between the human, dog and falcon was poetic, but you guys almost seem a little cult-like."

Robert smiled.

"It's metaphorical. All that attention to the sky helps keep us from falling off the earth."

She poured him some wine and they sat down at the kitchen table.

"So is chemistry your career?"

"Not exactly."

They talked for an hour. Ressa had grown up in Seattle and spent many summers on Vancouver Island and some of the islands off British Columbia. She learned about native culture from her father, who was an anthropologist. She fell in love with the bold designs and color of the Northwest native artwork and artifacts. She got her degrees in environmental chemistry and became an expert in historical analysis, restoration and preservation of art and artifacts. Sam's firm hired her as a consultant because it became obvious as they were preparing land use surveys that they not only needed to take into account the impact on animal and plant species, they had to be aware of the rich native heritage impact. Most of the surveys were done in the good weather of the summer. Ressa loved the fieldwork and since she consulted with different museums, she had some flexibility in her scheduling and took the job. It was clear as they talked that somehow Jane had told Ressa more about Robert than the other way around. The more she talked, the more fascinated he became. He did get his chance to explain his marriage break-up without going into details.

"I'm just going to make something quick and easy for dinner. You're welcome to have some."

"I would love to, but I have to take care of my animals. Plus I have some office work I must do tonight. Is there any way I could take a rain check and we could have dinner, say Friday?" Robert was practically begging.

"Ok."

"Fantastic! We can go after I take care of Sam's birds." Robert hadn't felt this good in a long time. The next few days flew by for him. There were no problems at the office, no emergency calls from Sean. On Friday Robert drove up to Sam's, took care of the birds and went to the house to get Ressa. She was dressed and ready to go. When he saw her with her hair loose in a simple, elegant dress, he couldn't help himself. He just blurted out, "You are really beautiful," as if he was talking to himself.

"Thank you."

There was something unusual in how she took things. She didn't feign shyness with the compliment or brush it off too quickly. She listened, took it to heart and responded. There was a pleasing naturalness to conversations with her. She was not thinking about being clever or the next thing she wanted to say, which in a strange way made the person talking to her a little more thoughtful. Robert had noticed that if someone was really listening, it made him want to make them understand. He clarified his own thoughts, became his own filter. The order of his exposition had to match the level of their attention. It became transforming. When your words have value to that person, you have value.

"You look very nice yourself, you know," she continued, as if she had to remind him that there was something mutual going on.

Over dinner, she asked about Maggie. Robert gave her a brief sketch. He didn't want to avoid the topic, but he had learned one thing over the years: if you are out with a woman, no matter what they ask or say, don't talk about another woman even if it's your mother or your sister, if you ever want to go out with her again.

"She sounds impressive."

"I think that's accurate, but I'm not sure that's the most important quality you need in a friend." Robert gave her a polite chance to talk about her relationships. She graciously kept it short. She had never married and there was no one at the moment. The conversation turned to art and they both became much more animated. They somehow got onto a topic where Robert told her he had an interesting young patient and that the cultural background of his dreams was not modern. There were no video games or science fiction but horses, eagles and coldness. He was always careful about the privacy of his patients, but they were talking about abstractions. She thought maybe the person got it through traveling. Robert assured her that couldn't be the source. She reminded him of the strong similarities in primitive art, art that had occurred simultaneously around the globe from peoples who could not possibly have influenced each other. Physically, it was almost impossible to explain, but there were other theories that these mutual arisings might have occurred from a pool of collective unconscious. Robert liked her thinking. It was clear and she was very smart. At one point they came around to talking about textile art and she began talking about fabrics. To explain a point, she wanted to show the feel of a cloth. If the average person was going to feel the fabric of someone's pants, they would probably reach down near the ankle where the material would be loose from the skin and far enough toward some extremity so as not to be too sexual, but she felt his thigh. She was intellectual, she knew how to handle ideas with her mind, but she also had to know things directly with her senses. She made Robert feel comfortable with her touch. It had been a long time since anyone had touched him that way.

Sam and Jane and the girls were going to be back over the weekend. Robert asked where she lived and she gave him her address and phone number. They didn't have to wait long to see each other again because as soon as the Lindley's all arrived back home, Jane wanted to have a thank you dinner. She had brought back some little gifts for Robert and Ressa and invited them for dinner the following week.

Chapter Thirteen

Reentry From the Bardo

"As rebirth approaches, you crave more and more for the support of the material body."
—Sogyal Rinpoche

When Sean came in for his session, Robert knew they were in a different place. It was a vulnerable place, and they were not finished yet. After some small talk, Robert asked Sean how it had been going.

"Ok," he said, not very enthusiastically.

"Are you still practicing?"

"Yes, I'm pretty good at it." Robert smiled at his confidence.

"Dr. Rob, I am tired of living in my head." He had taken Robert a little by surprise.

"It just seems I'm always worried about what I'm going to start thinking."

"Is it always scary or upsetting? Do you mean like apprehension because something bad will come up?"

"No. Well, sometimes. But it's like waiting for something to happen. I can't seem to get out of it. It's not always bad."

"Does it seem like daydreaming? Has your mother or anyone at school noticed and said anything or flat out asked or accused you of daydreaming?"

"Yes, but not all the time."

"Sean, I have to tell you that I don't know how you learned to make the perfect imitation of an eagle, nor where your knowledge of horses comes from. I don't know and I would be leery of anyone who told me for sure they know, but I know these things are real. I can't tell you, 'you were here' in some geographical place and that's where you learned it, but I know the place in a different way and maybe it's an even more important way. If you show me a picture of a prison, I might not be able to tell you that the prison is in Detroit, Michigan, but I know what a prison is. I know what it's for, and I know what goes on in prisons. I know some of the things people have to do to get into a prison. I am convinced something pretty awful happened to you and you have an awareness of it. I also think it was the cause of your fears of abandonment, but I am convinced it is over. Remember when we talked about the wood in a fire changing to heat, smoke, ash and light? You have changed. Some people never seem to change. They act the same way day in and day out until they die. Then they have to change. Other people show big changes. Something big happens to them and they are different. Some work for a lifetime to practice to be better human beings. They change more slowly. You are not the wood anymore, but you are not all smoke and light. I don't think that process is complete. The wood is still becoming something else. I think that is what is going on right now with you. I think in the next couple weeks, you will become more secure in the new you and I'm betting a lot of the confusion will disappear."

Sean listened intently.

"But this time now is very important. We need to work hard not to step back, that's why the practice is so important. We can't go back to the old ways. It might be comfortable to be near your mother all the time but it's not healthy. You can control those impulses. You already are seeing you can control some of your thoughts. We can get better and you will love your freedom. Am I making any sense?"

"Yes." Sean seemed calm, accepting. There wasn't the anxiety, the heaviness of the dread.

"So you have to keep your mind in check and always remember

I am here to help. I would like you to start thinking of some things you would like to do physically, like maybe start playing a sport. I don't know, but think about it. It doesn't have to be tomorrow, but by next week I'd like to know some things that you might be interested in. I think we can get you out of your head. I'll try to help. Try to make a list, ok?'

Sean nodded his agreement.

"It's not a rush," Robert soothed him, "we need to make good choices. Sean, you have made great strides in facing your fears. I think so much of the difficulties you have endured have been the cost of those fears having so much control and never being addressed. You have broken through in the last weeks. You have to also remember you're doing all this without any drugs. I think some of the fogginess is from the chemicals in your body readjusting."

Robert and Sean talked a little more. Robert wanted to make sure Sean knew he would be there if Sean needed him, but it was good he wasn't right there at his side all week, that he was learning to solve immediate crises himself. When Robert went back out to the waiting room with Sean, Patricia Nelson was there. She wanted Robert to know she felt important changes in Sean. Robert said he was excited but wanted to remain cautiously optimistic. They were breaking the surface. Now was not the time to be complacent. He told her of the list he wanted Sean to begin to work on. Sean was Robert's last patient of the day. He was already thinking of dinner tomorrow at Sam and Jane's. He was excited to see everyone.

When Robert pulled in Sam and Jane's driveway for the thank you dinner, he could see Ressa's jeep was already there. When he walked in the kitchen door, Jane, Ressa and Carly were all in the kitchen. Sam was in the living room, putting more wood on the fire. Carly got to Robert first and kissed him. He lifted her up with a big hug.

"Are we going to play a little tonight?"

"Yes, if you want to."

"Absolutely."

Jane came in behind her and gave him an old friend's kiss and hug. She kept it short because she wanted to introduce Ressa and not make her feel uncomfortably left out.

"Robert, this is Ressa Ferrin."

"Yes," Robert answered. He looked coyly at Ressa. "We have met."

Ressa walked over and they kissed politely, which didn't go unnoticed by Jane. Ressa said hello to Robert as Sam came in from the other room. Sam and Robert shook hands and Robert teased them how about how tan they all were. Finally, the other two girls came in and hugged Robert. Sam asked if Robert wanted a glass of wine.

"Love one. Did I do a good job with the birds?"

"Perfect, thank you very much. You've met Ressa?"

Simultaneously, Robert and Jane said, "Yes."

Jane added, "They've met." Only Sam could have noticed her tone.

Under his breath he softly said, "Ok," wondering, what was that about.

At dinner, Robert was in good form, teasing the girls, asking about their trip. Ressa sat across from him, the girls around him, Sam at one end of the table and Jane at the other. Sam told Robert and Ressa about the breeding operation Bernardo had. Jane brought out beautifully wrapped little gifts for Robert and Ressa. Sam and Jane genuinely thanked them, wanting them to understand that the only way that they felt they could all go and have a nice time without worrying about the ranch was because of Robert and Ressa.

After dinner everyone helped clear the table, but the girls had it all sorted out in short order and they were soon all sitting in the living room. Ressa sat on the sofa and Robert sat in a chair about ten feet away. He had a hard time not looking at her. He didn't want to be obvious, but in the rhythm of the conversation, especially if she was speaking, he had the perfect excuse to stare at her. Sometimes what she was saying didn't register, he was so transfixed by her. He couldn't stop himself from comparing Maggie and Ressa. He began daydreaming.

Maggie's attractiveness and beauty was acculturated. You had to be trained to really get it, he thought. You had to know the brands of clothes, the fit, the fabrics, the style of her hair, the different ways she wore it and when. You would have to recognize the names of the schools she attended, you had to know how they ranked socially and academically, and you should really have known who had ranked them. It was interesting that all it seemed to take was to train someone to recognize these things and then that awareness would automatically infuse them with importance. Augustine only seemed to need to show Maggie power and it interested her, to say nothing of being in those schools with those other kids trained to recognize the same things, competing for status and achievement. It could set up a lifetime of habits. If you are not careful, your own natural definitions get tampered with. At three years old a child can understand empathy. It can take thirty more years for a social group to develop controls over it. The question becomes how much of your appreciation has been trained into you. One day, you find yourself making an excuse or explaining what a friend is wearing or where they live, the car they drive or how they hold a fork and you act like you don't mean it but you do. Things have backfired. Instead of the sophistication opening you up, exclusivity has locked you in. Robert was just watching Ressa when a cold shudder went through his body. What if the ghost he had been feeling coming back was her?

Finally, Carly broke the spell and got Robert to play with her. They had fun with a couple pieces, then Robert asked her to play by herself, something special or something that was her own personal favorite. She played Bach. This was a young girl raised in the West with hunters and horse people. Robert marveled how Jane and Sam managed to expose the girls to art and even get them to enjoy it so much. When Carly finished everyone clapped, Robert the loudest. He insisted on an encore and she played a technical piece by Chopin. At the end the response was quieter but even more seriously appreciative. Now it was her turn, so she asked Robert to play a couple of his favorites and everyone was with her. With the guitar in his hands, Robert felt in control. He played a Spanish piece that was cheerful and flamboyant. If the others noticed they didn't seem to let on, but the musician in Carly was curious. She was unusually impressed with his playing. Jane noticed the expression on Carly's face. For the second piece he'd play one for his and Ressa's roots, a Gaelic piece that his father had taught him and was one of his mother's favorites. He began to play more and more lyrically. Jane knew the other girls were too young, but watching Carly's face, Jane knew she was going to have some explaining to do.

Jane and Sam were in bed. Sam had his eyes closed. There was only the dim light from Jane's reading lamp. She spoke quietly to her apparently sleeping husband.

"How do you think that went?"

"You're not talking about the food, are you?" he mumbled.

Jane reached under the covers and pinched Sam on the butt.

"Hey!" he jumped, laughing.

"You noticed," Jane insisted.

"Noticed what?"

"When he played the guitar. He hasn't played like that, ever. I think she was taken."

"I wouldn't overthink it."

"I'm not overthinking it. You didn't see when he came in. She kissed him. They already knew each other."

"Honey, if it's true, that's great. Robert needs some fun. He hasn't had much in a while."

Ressa loved the guitar but she was more taken that night by Robert's play with the kids and their reactions to him. She thought she might like to be part of that.

Chapter Fourteen

Born Again

O now, when the Birthplace Bardo upon me is dawning!
Abandoning idleness – there being no idleness ... in life –
Entering into the Reality undistractedly, listening, reflecting, and meditating,
Carrying on to the path [knowledge of the true nature of] appearances and of mind,
May the Tri-Kaya be realized:
Once that the human form hath been attained,
May there be no time [or opportunity] in which to idle it [or human life] away.
—The Tibetan Book of the Dead

It was still very cold, but the days were getting slightly longer again. It was noticeable and the little extra light seemed to make everyone feel better. Robert had heard from Maggie. He did miss her and when he heard her voice he wanted to soften and be warmer, but her astringent tone seemed to clarify their relationship and future. She was going to come back west during the school's spring break. They could sort out the details and finalize the divorce. Robert told her that would be fine, he would do whatever needed to be done on the western end. For now at least, he'd like to stay in the house, so he would have it appraised and if she agreed, he'd buy her half. They could go over the furniture, etcetera, when she came out. That sounded fine with her.

It was Sean's last week of the planned intensive treatment. Robert was feeling reflective, cautious. As soon as Robert saw Sean when he came for his appointment, he felt good. Sean was at least for the time being off all medications. He was shaky, but panic wasn't one step away. After some small talk, they were going to go over "the list" and begin to talk about where to go from here, but somehow they got on the subject of fear.

"Sean, we can't avoid fear or ignore it. You have to try to examine it so you can put it in its place and go on living." Robert tried to explain to him that a great problem now would be fear, fear of the dreams, fear of situations with other kids and people, and that all the kinds of frightening objects were not the most important thing. It was to stay ahead of the cycle of fear. They rehearsed their behavior techniques as they always did. Robert coached him like an athlete. He wanted to make sure his responses would keep working, reflexively.

Sean interrupted Robert.

"Dr. Rob, I'll tell you what I am afraid of." His tone caught Robert and focused his attention.

"What's that?"

"I'm afraid I might do something stupid again that will upset everybody and ruin everything."

Robert had to fight back some tears. Sean had gotten to him. There was a quick flood of emotion and he instinctively hugged the boy.

"Sean, you never did anything stupid before. You did something people didn't understand. It made them afraid. It was never your fault." Robert held the boy for a little while, then he sat down in front of him. He wanted him to see his face.

"Sean, I don't like fear. Of course, I have a whole set of my own fears and they cause a lot of trouble when they get the upper hand in my decisions. This is all so much of the core of what we have been working on. Do you see that?"

"I think so."

"It's really important that you see those incidents were not your fault. They were out of your control."

"I get that."

"Sean, all animals will fight back if they are cornered and there is no way out. That can be a legitimate response to threat, but too many people build walls around themselves to protect themselves from every threat and the same walls become a trap. People add to them, building them higher and higher. The protection is a prison. They get angry, defending all the time, and the anger and fear are addictive. They can't do anything fun because they're locked in. Sean, you had one of your biggest fears of aloneness and a few weeks ago you bravely faced that fear and there out in some place where there were no people, you said you weren't lonely. The loneliness, the aloneness were gone. I don't think you were ever afraid of other people not being around. I think it was losing yourself. The aloneness can be separate from people. You know I like falconry, right? Well, the grouse always know the falcon is a threat, but they don't build fortresses to keep the falcons out. If they did, they would stop living the life of grouse. Death is a part of life. Too many people bury themselves way too early. The message of falconry is the uncertainty of the outcome. If death is inevitable, why don't we just die now and save all the bother? Because you would miss all the excitement of living on this wonderful, mysterious planet. You have a long life ahead of you. The falcon is always there. That is what it is to be human, but we can have a lot of amazing experiences in the meantime."

"Can we talk about the list of things you might like to do? Did anything come to mind?"

Sean seemed a little hesitant, so Robert tried to prompt him.

"What about horses? You have an affinity with horses. Did you ever think of riding lessons?"

"I don't really like horses. Horses got me into a lot of trouble."

Robert caught the tone and had to smile.

"It was just a suggestion. Ok, something else."

Finally, almost as if it were a secret, Sean said quietly, "Soccer."

"Soccer." He was a little surprised. That was easy, he thought to himself.

"That's great! You know, there is a good program at school and there's a club. There are some very good coaches."

Sean nodded.

Robert didn't want to push, but he assured Sean it was something they could pursue. He would talk to his mother and see what the spring schedule looked like and see about tryouts. When Robert talked to Patricia Nelson after Sean's appointment, she told him Sean had posters of all the great soccer players, he followed the world league and knew all the teams. Robert had no idea. They were both optimistic.

Later in the week, Ressa invited Robert to the little house she rented. It was tidy, but the most striking feature of the house was her collection of masks. She told Robert that they were a few of her favorites. She had more back in storage in Seattle. Robert liked them. The Tibetan masks he knew could be so ferocious and intimidating and at the moment he was a little sensitive about them. The African masks he had seen were frightening and violent voodoo arts, but these masks were not contorted human faces. They were of many animals and different themes and the carving was at a high level. Some with shaved tan cedar strips for hair and all of them painted in bold colors. It was easy to see the influence of the sea islands. The striking black and white patterns of the killer whales, the strong curves of the eagle's beaks, the greens of frogs, the bright reds of the salmon and the blue of the sky and streams. That could be learned from books, but unless you had been there for a while you needed someone to explain to you what it could be like to live half blind in a shroud of fog for days or have most of your sight be blocked by weeks of rain only to have it clear from time to time, sometimes in a matter of minutes to this unbelievable scenery that had been surrounding you all the time. To one side, the ocean and whales and salmon coming from the ocean up into the purest rivers and streams, on the other side snowcapped mountains and trees as large as anywhere in the world, ravens and eagles. You needed someone knowledgeable to guide you into the mystery of a place with exaggerated weather and geography settled by very strong people, part of the Paleo-Siberian migration eastward along the arctic coast by Eskimo and along the northwest coast by Indians. If you needed someone to guide you through the physical landscape, then you certainly needed someone to guide you into a mental landscape that could produce huge, exaggerated totemic art and simultaneously shut people in for such long periods of time that their expressions would be tiny, exquisite surgical sculpting as tight and perfect as the tightest orchestra, not a single flaw in all the intricate notes. It was no wonder that this manic place had produced some the greatest shamans in the world.

Over dinner, she told him some of the mythic stories behind the main characters in the masks. She showed him some of the jewelry she had, carvings in silver by the Haida and Kwaikutel. She was a good storyteller and he felt transported to a magical place.

She had a small fireplace and after dinner they both sat down on the couch in front of it.

"You know," he said, "you frightened me a little."

"Why?"

"It was partially the feeling of being captivated by you. I felt such a rush. I mean, look at the way we met. That was unusual. Pretty dramatic. Then, I see all these masks. I spend most of my time trying to get people to take them off. You grew up in this naturally powerful place where people easily put them on. You're comfortable in that wild weather and geography. Maybe you're some kind of shaman." He was teasing a little.

"Robert, you know very well that what makes a shaman is someone else's belief, not the shaman's. What's going on? Am I pushing too hard? Am I making you nervous?"

"I am nervous, but you're not pushing too hard."

She leaned closer to him to feel him.

"Robert, what are you nervous about?"

"I think it's falling in love, with the emphasis on falling."

She had a slight smile on her face. She wanted him to continue, to explain. She was feeling a little anxious, wondering if he was looking for a way out.

"I mean, a person doesn't plan to trip and fall down the stairs. It just happens and sometimes it hurts badly. For me, it didn't always fit in nice, neat consecutive time frames. I think, at least before Maggie, I fell in love more easily. Maybe too easily. I know some of my friends tried to convince me that I was irresponsible, but I never saw it that way. I thought love was so rare that if you ever had the chance for it to happen to you, you had to go for it. I loved the feeling of being in love. I wasn't recklessly drawn to the flames of passion. It was at least as much that I was living with the fear of dying a long, slow death in the prison of propriety and reason. My work was showing me the holes in what people like to call rational thinking and free will. I wasn't convinced we had the control of our lives that people thought we did. Maybe I bought the criticism or advice, maybe I did what a lot of people do and transferred that energy to my job, maybe I was using Maggie as an example. I don't think that is true. I tried to fall in love with Maggie over and over. That's the part where things have to happen that are not necessarily in your control. I got comfortable making excuses for it. Now I'm not used to these other feelings, so they make me nervous."

"Don't you think that a lot of this is coming from the place where you are right now? I don't want you to feel anxious about being with me. If you need a little more space to get through all this - ."

He interrupted her. "No, I don't need more space. I need the opposite, but I think I'm a little afraid of it. I think part of what looks like confusion is, but I'm not at all confused about how I feel about you."

He stopped for a second, playing back his own remarks in his head.

"Are you sure you want to go out with a psychiatrist?"

She looked at him with a smile, slightly teasing, as if to say I'm not sure.

"Robert, can we just be two people enjoying each other's company for now?"

He nodded.

"Would you like a drink?"

"Absolutely."

She poured two glasses of wine and sat back down next to him, feeling more comfortable now.

"Do you want to see what I think is the most amazing artwork from where I grew up?" She thought it was probably time to lighten things up.

She brought out a book of painting and photographs. She moved closer to him so they both could see it together. In the middle of the talking she gracefully lifted her long leg as if it were part of a choreographed ballet and softly laid it over his. A dancer practices and practices, then refines the practice with so much control that the effort is invisible to the audience. The symbolic intention of the choreographer comes through so subtly that the audience wonders if there was any. They only grasp or gasp at the effect of the story. It felt so good to him. She was explaining a photograph when he stopped her, he wanted to say one more thing. He looked at her and realized that whatever he had wanted to say was not important. She looked at his face for what seemed like a very long time, then slowly leaned toward him and kissed him. It reminded him of slow dances in high school where he got closer and closer, hormones on fire, drugged by the scents of a girl's hair. He stayed over at her house until morning.

CHAPTER FIFTEEN

Preparing for Spring

A few days later, Robert was in the office when he got a call from Sam. He was in town and just on a chance he wondered if Robert was free to have lunch with him. Robert told him yes, it would work, so they met at a diner where it was quiet. Sam was not the kind of person who could play games with small talk, so he got right to the point.

"Robert, I know you know that Maggie is coming in a few weeks and Jane wants her to stay with us while she is here. I just wanted to see how you feel about it, face to face. I will say she wanted me to tell you that if somehow the tables were turned, she would insist you stay with us."

"Thanks for being up front. I have no problems with that at all. Frankly, I'm grateful because I was thinking about moving out of the house for the days she is here and offering it to her, but this is much better. This way she won't be alone. It's going to be a little stressful splitting up some of the stuff. She'll have you guys for support. Did you talk to her? Is it ok with her?"

"Well, we just heard from Maggie which dates she would be here. To be honest, Jane gave me twenty four hours to talk to you." Sam rolled his eyes. "That's why I'm here."

"I wondered about the lunch thing," Robert teased. "No, seriously. I think it's good. My conversations with her are a little tense and edgy. I don't want there to be trouble. Knowing that you guys are involved might make us behave better. You know, I don't have any ill will toward her at all."

Their conversation turned toward falconry. When they got up to leave, Robert insisted on paying. As they split up on the street, Robert shook Sam's hand strongly, thanking him for thinking about his feelings and making a special trip to see him. Sam looked at him in a self-effacing way to diminish the gesture and said in a funny tone, "You know, it couldn't have gone any other way," giving a nod to Jane's power in running the house. Robert laughed as they walked away from each other.

When Sam got back home, Jane was in the kitchen.

"What are we going to tell the girls?" Jane asked.

"They already know they're split up. I don't think we need to go any deeper right now."

"I'm not talking about that, what I'm talking about is Robert and Ressa. I don't want that to come up while she's here going through everything else. Carly knows something is up."

"So we talk to Carly. We're here to support both of them. They are both friends of our family. These things happen. Their personal lives are not our business and we're not going to bring up anything that might make either one of them uncomfortable, period."

Jane was already thinking it wasn't going to be as easy as that.

"Well," she said, "we have some time. I'll talk to her. She really loves Robert."

Sam looked at her through the upper part of his glasses. "All the women love Robert," he said. She laughed.

"Honey, are you sure this is all about Carly?"

"What do you mean?"

"Maybe you don't like someone showing interest in your best friend's ex-husband?"

"That's not it." She said it in a way that wasn't convincing, even to her herself.

The next time Robert saw Sean for his appointment it was clear

Sean had undergone a monumental change. Robert was not used to this kind of recovery. This was more the experience of some of his other friends in medicine. Someone needs a hip replaced; the next day he is walking and in weeks he is back riding his bike or horse. A person is on the verge of a bursting appendix; in the face of a painful death from peritonitis, the surgeon removes it, she walks away perfect. It wasn't like that in psychiatry. Injure the brain or psyche and that person may think with a limp until the day they die. He kept thinking about being comfortable in the not knowing, but how would that read up on the wall with the diplomas? Welcome, I don't understand a lot of what I am doing, but I might be able to find a way to help you. That would be good for business!

Robert and Sean went over again the necessity of keeping up work on their practices, staying on top of fear, the personal control. Robert warned him that things would come up in sport and in school that might test him, but to remember that they would be more preparations for life.

"Sean, we've been through a lot. For you, it's been a lifetime of habits. You have to remember that things will come up. You might feel that you're falling back, but you'll see the feelings won't have the intensity. We've kind of taken the heart out of the beast. It may bluster, but it won't have that kind of power over you anymore. One thing I want to make very clear and this is between you and me. If you ever need to talk, I'll be available. Keep the phone I gave you for a while. Here is a card with my phone number on it. Put it somewhere in case you ever need it. I think you are looking so good that we don't have to meet every week anymore. I'd like to stretch it out to every other week and see where it goes from there. What do you think?"

"I think that's ok."

"You're clear that this is not me kicking you out in any way, right?"

"Yes."

"You're better. I'm a doctor. My work is done." He squeezed Sean's shoulder.

They finished on an upbeat feeling, with Robert assuring Sean that he'd come to some practices and soccer games. Robert was so encouraged at the end of the appointment that when he met with Patricia Nelson he suggested that they spread the appointments out to every two weeks and then make a gradual tapering off. It was a tightrope for Robert. He wanted to make a substantive gesture to recognize the progress, but he didn't want to put a strain on what was new and fragile. The more time that passed now with Sean in control of his own life, the more stress he would be able to endure. Patricia had tears in her eyes. Robert and Sean looked at each other as if they both had to reassure Patricia. Robert reiterated that he was not saying goodbye in any way and that he wanted to know the soccer practice schedule so he could drop in and catch a few. He would see them in two weeks.

Ressa had never been to Robert's house. In the days before her visit, Robert found himself in a quandary. Maggie would be here in a couple of weeks. They would have to have some serious meetings about dividing the possessions. He didn't want to take down all the photographs of Maggie and Maggie and Augustine and Maggie and the horses and all of them in New York, but Ressa was coming over and he didn't need to feel like he was inviting her into Maggie's bedroom. In the end, he did take down a few things that he could put back before Maggie came, but he left most of them. It would be odd. He hoped Ressa would understand. A few more weeks and things would be more settled.

He started making dinner for them. When Ressa arrived, he showed her the animals first. She loved Griffin. She thought his black and white colors and long, fine coat were beautiful and Griffin followed her everywhere. Finally, they got to the house. Robert felt he had to explain why he left things as they were when Maggie left. Ressa understood and actually told him that it was thoughtful. While Robert was putting the finishing touches on the meal, Ressa wandered around the house. She stopped and examined the photographs of Maggie. She came back into the kitchen to help him. She leaned on him and hugged him gently.

"She's beautiful. Are you sure you know what you are doing?"

"I'm sure," he answered, and for a moment he almost broke his rule and was going to talk about her to Ressa, but he didn't. That could come later. His hands were wet from the sink. He wanted to touch her to reassure her so he looked at her, looked at his hands and kissed her instead. She smiled widely.

"Would you mind opening that wine?" he pointed with his head while he was drying his hands.

If the dinner at her house was a chance to hear about her, then tonight at his house it could be more of his biography. She liked his stories. He had inherited his Scottish sense of humor from his father and he was having fun finding ways to make her laugh. They were settling in after dinner. Robert wanted to tell her something that had been bothering him and he wanted to know what she thought. He didn't want to scare her off, but he had been worrying about their age difference.

"Ressa, I like you. I mean, I really like you. But it keeps going through my mind, what if it worked out and we got together and we stayed together? What would happen when I'm decrepit and I have nothing to offer? It would be logical for someone your age to try to find someone more exciting."

Ressa looked at him and gently said, "How can a falconer ask that question? Every day you send that bird off on its own, free. You give it the option to fly off, but you must have made a place where it would rather be because it comes back."

"Sometimes they fly off."

"Then what do you do?"

"We chase them down with telemetry!" They both burst out laughing.

"Robert, I don't know how two people think they can predict the future, but I hear it all the time. 'I can't do this,' because I know how it will end up. How do they know? Of course they don't, but they beat down chance with the hammer of their own projections. Is it fear in general? A fear of losing control? You probably know better. How will you let life happen, how will you know what might be? The irony I see is that the attempts at control do work, but not in the way people think. They don't control a situation or control fate, they just block it out and don't let it happen. To me, that isn't experiencing a life or living a life. That's the opposite. It's shutting down a life. You said you were afraid. I think we're all afraid, unless you're a fool, but I try to stop beating down passion. The interesting thing to me is the more educated I became, the more I kept coming back, understanding, trusting more primitive advice. It doesn't matter how sophisticated you think it is, it's always primitive, primal. What makes someone go out into the ocean in a fog after a whale in a canoe? It's too easy to be patronizing and call it desperation or primitive stupidity. It's not stupidity. It's the courage to approach risk, acknowledge chance and go anyway. The practicality comes in not before the decision, but after. I'm going, but how can I make it back alive? There will never be enough information around to make the outcome a certainty. I didn't really learn that in statistics and probability classes. In the end, it will always be a leap of faith. If you don't let go, your own life, your own destiny, can't get a piece of you. So maybe it is like your falconry. You work on yourself, do things right. Unlock the birds, see if they want to come back, but all we can do is really answer to ourselves. You can't control the falcon. Make me always want to be around you, like I do now, and I will try to do the same for you."

He was quiet. He just looked at her with a smile, impressed. They skipped dessert and went from the living room to the bedroom. During the middle of the night, he woke up and looked at her sleeping peacefully. He thought, what is wrong with me? I've spent the better part of the last six months tangled up farther in the past than I ever thought was possible. It played a considerable part in the dissolution of my marriage and now just into a new and amazing relationship, my mind is catapulting me right past the present into obsessions about the future. He took a deep breath and then another. Again, he told himself.

CHAPTER SIXTEEN

Maggie's Visit

Jane picked up Maggie from the airport. They were happy to see each other. Maggie felt the air was colder, but it did feel lighter and cleaner. There were tiny glimpses of spring, even though winter could hang around for a while longer out here. On the way from the airport, Jane quizzed Maggie about the job. In a humble way, Maggie acknowledged the workload but told Jane about some of the famous people she routinely had to deal with. Jane didn't want her to be humble. They were good friends. She wanted all the gossip, if it was important. She could see Maggie was excited and impressed. When things settled more, Maggie wanted Jane to come east for some visits. There was plenty of room at the farm. They could ride or shop in New York. The girls had to come and they needed to see the schools now, so they could start thinking about the future. She told Jane that she and Augustine and Johnny were working on a way for her to spend more time on the farm. They wanted her to eventually take over the big house. Johnny had bought a place in Florida and he and Augustine were going to try to spend some time there in the winters. They would move into the small stone cottage on the farm. So much had happened in a few months. When they got to the ranch, Sam and the girls greeted her warmly. All their excitement was slightly tempered by the reason for the visit, but they had all been lectured not to dwell on that. They had a nice meal and

Jane and Maggie stayed up pretty late talking. Finally the jet lag and upcoming itinerary got to Maggie and she thought she'd better get to bed. She had to meet Robert around ten the next morning.

Robert was at home. It was early in the evening on Friday. Knowing Maggie was in town made him slightly anxious. Their future seemed clear, but there were still mixed feelings, memories that kept swinging into his head. He wanted to be with Ressa or at least call her but they had agreed to give each other some room for the next couple days so Robert could get through this. Robert's secretary Marilyn had told him that her son and Sean's older brother played on a basketball team together and that she heard Sean's brother had convinced Sean to play on the junior team. Tonight was a game, so Robert was glad he had something to do to take his mind off Maggie and their meeting tomorrow.

When Robert got to the gym, he had hardly gotten through the door when James Nelson spotted him from up in a section of bleachers. He waved to Robert and Robert made his way over. The place wasn't crowded but it was not surprisingly empty. He sat down next to James. They were by themselves. Robert explained that Marilyn's son played with James' older son and that's how he heard Sean was playing. James pointed down to the bench. Sean was sitting with his back to Robert and James.

"The coach lets them all play. They're shortened games, but Sean will play a little."

"Great."

James told Robert how thankful he was. It had been going on a long time and to see this change in Sean was wonderful. They shook hands firmly. There was no need for many more words.

"We'll just have to keep a watch on the situation, but my hope is that he will continue to get better and better."

"He thinks a lot of you, Doc."

"He's a great kid. I knew about his thing with soccer but I didn't know about the basketball."

"It just happened. Richard, our oldest, kind of talked him into it. They both apparently got the height from my side of the family.

Richard told him he was sure they would play him, so he was ok with it. We were thrilled."

About then, Sean turned around to see his Dad. He was going in to play. He hadn't seen Robert come in, so when he looked to his Dad he was almost shocked to see Robert, but a big smile quickly came over his face. Robert gave him two cheering thumbs up. Into the game he went.

The little game was infectious with its own dramas, shoes untied, awkward play and over-jealous parents and Robert was completely absorbed by it. For a little while, he was free of the drama in his own life. He stayed for a bit after Sean played and had a chance to give him a congratulatory wave before he left. James was going to stay for Richard's game. As Robert drove home, he felt a calmness as if for the first time he really believed that their work together may have paid off. Something serious had changed. He felt the remaining sessions with Sean would be more conventional. He still hadn't put the whole thing together, but there was a comforting, mystical taste that had completely permeated the medical part. It was the same feeling as when he walked into a big forest with giant trees. He never felt diminished or threatened. It was just the opposite. It was the same comforting feeling of being part of something much bigger than himself. He was trying to imagine what a feat and what an experience it was for young Sean to be so consciously out in those spaces. To have been there as a witness was one thing, but it was another to navigate. Starting there so young, where would he end up?

In the morning, Maggie drove over to the house in one of Sam and Jane's cars. When he saw her pull up, Robert let Griffin out of the door. He bounded up to Maggie's car and when Maggie got out he went wild, twisting himself in knots around her legs, wagging his tail so hard it hurt when it hit her leg. She loved the welcome. Robert could see the smile on her face from the house door. She walked up the path to the house and he walked down to meet her. They kissed politely, but when they hugged each other, Robert thought he felt some earnest emotion and it made him feel more at ease. They went into the house. Maggie glanced around. Everything looked the same, which was somehow comforting, but faintly, very faintly, she smelled another woman. She knew he had realtors and appraisers, so she dismissed it. He had coffee made; they sat down in the kitchen and started. There were a few pleasantries, but they pretty much started right in. He did have the house appraised and he would like to stay in it if he could. If she agreed with the appraisal, he would like to buy out her half. If they agreed on the basics, a lawyer could finalize it. For the next couple hours, they went through the house. Robert made a careful list of everything she wanted. He would get some professional movers to do it all at once. They both agreed to have it all spelled out so the lawyers would just facilitate. Neither one of them had any reason for argument over any of their assets. It was time for lunch by the time they were through. Robert asked her if she would like to have lunch in town. She agreed, she still had to go over the logistics of having her other horses shipped and her tack. Tomorrow night, she planned to cook for the Lindley's as a thank you and then it would be back east Monday morning.

At lunch she told him about the new job. That was familiar. What was so strange to him was to have lunch with someone he had had a thousand meals with, he thought to himself. You know she hates paper napkins and she uses one without the slightest hesitation. How did you lose the familiarity? You've slept together for years and now you are self-conscious if there is a speck of food on your face. Before, she would have reached over and brushed your cheek without even interrupting the conversation and you wouldn't have even moved your head, you trusted her so completely. How does a couple escort themselves out of the most intimate existence to this level of asinine formality? It's done all the time, he knew, and now it was happening to him. He wanted to say, do you know who I am? Of course she knows, but people make the decision that their bodies are not available to each other anymore. Touch is taken out of the equation, but it's not necessarily just the physical touch. It's the space, Robert thought. Two people can be far apart and yet they move easily through the space in between and feel close, and two people can stand right next to each other in space as impenetrable as concrete.

The real crime is not that you go on to another life or love, he thought. The real crime is that two people force themselves and each other to nullify and diminish what they had. They get angry or do things to make the other person angry. They fall into depressions with enough gravity to pull in everything around them. They scare people. Without even thinking, they hunt for a push or pull to get out of the orbit they are stuck in. It doesn't have to be diminished. It already has diminished, maybe all by itself. Maybe everyone is to blame and maybe no one is to blame. It is just being held together by ritual, a very powerful narcotic habit. Only when the longing, like that of some immigrant for his homeland, reaches a point where you miss something so much, will you then take a chance, even a stupid chance, to try to get back to a place you know exists. We don't need diminishment to let go, he thought, we need some desperation.

Finally, Robert broke out of the business rhythm of their conversation.

"Maggie why did we break up? Did we fall out of love?" He wanted to ask her, did you ever love me?

"Bobby," she sighed, and for a moment she seemed real and relaxed, "it takes more than love. We're too different as people. You look down on ambition."

He flinched visibly. Why did he go and get emotional?

"No, Bobby. You do. You think it's unsavory."

He wasn't going to argue. He tried to listen. It would have been futile. For Maggie, ambition was synonymous with hard work. Success was the ethical reward for the energy she put in to it. Robert saw hard work and success on different orbits. Sometimes they intersected, but it was so much about luck.

"Maggie, I've seen so many people work just as hard as another person, but they just seem to have bad luck. A wrong roll of the dice and the hard work and ambition doesn't pay off."

"Bobby, we make our own luck."

"Then maybe I feel like I'm always about to be unlucky, because when I see someone unluckily in bad straits, I think there by the grace of god go I."

Robert could feel the air draining out of his emotional gesture. There was not much glue, she was visibly losing interest in his talking. He got the message. They returned to regular conversation. He made her promise to give his best to Augustine and Johnny and invite them out for a trip anytime they wanted. Finally, they agreed to meet Monday morning for any last minute details before her flight out.

There was really only one large place to shop for groceries in town. On Saturday morning Maggie went to buy some things for the meal she was going to cook for Jane and Sam and the girls. Through some cosmological force, Ressa went in to shop at the same time and Patricia Nelson was there shopping for her family. Ressa had Maggie's image fresh in her mind from seeing the gallery of photographs of her in different settings at Robert's house, so when she saw this unusual woman, dressed so perfectly, her attention was galvanized from nearly across the store. She knew Maggie had no idea who she was, so with her curiosity tripped she meandered through the aisles to get a closer look. As she was walking through the store, she noticed that another woman had walked up to Maggie. Ressa kept nonchalantly pretend-shopping, closer and closer. The other woman was Patricia Nelson. She too had seen Maggie from way off. They had never met, but she was easy to recognize from pictures in the paper. By the time Patricia had reached Maggie, Ressa was close enough to hear their conversation.

Patricia walked up to Maggie. In a humble voice she said, "I really want to apologize for bothering you in public. I know we've never met, but I recognized you as Dr. Robert McPherson's wife."

Maggie tensed up and stood still. She didn't smile. She had no idea why this woman was approaching her or how much she knew about her and Robert's divorce. She spoke guardedly. Neither woman reached out her hand.

"I just felt I had to say something about how much our whole family feels indebted to your husband for his help with our son. We were at a dead end in his treatment. But with Dr. McPherson, my son has turned a complete corner to the point where he made the soccer team today. I know you don't know, but it is an amazing thing that I never foresaw happening."

Patricia had mist in her eyes and Maggie softened.

"I don't want to take any more of your time, but I had to tell you how wonderful your husband has been to us."

Ressa was fifteen feet away. She heard the conversation and although she knew nothing of the complexity of the story or the personalities, she couldn't help feeling warmed by the praise. By now, Maggie had realized who Patricia Nelson had to be. Politely reserved, she spoke to Patricia.

"Thank you. It's very nice to hear your son is better."

There was a brief moment after they parted when Maggie stopped shopping. Standing motionless, still holding some grocery item in her hand, her eyes scanned up from her thoughts the way people will stare at someone when they are talking on the phone. Her eyes looked right at Ressa. Ressa looked back at her and then turned to finish her shopping.

Ressa had planned to give Robert some space over the weekend, but after she got home later in the afternoon, she decided to give him a quick call to see how he was holding up.

"Hi."

"Hi." He was glad to hear her voice.

"I won't keep you - I was just thinking about you and had to see how you were doing."

"I'm fine. Had a good meeting with Maggie yesterday. Settled pretty much everything. She's at the Lindley's. They're all having a dinner together. I was just going to go out and get something to eat. I don't feel like cooking."

"Lonely?"

He laughed.

"I was supposed to give you some time to yourself, but I was shopping today and bought some nice fish. Do you want to come over for something very simple?"

"Sure! I can be there in an hour."

When he got to Ressa's, she was busy preparing dinner. She asked him if he would mind starting a fire. When the fire was crackling, he went back to the kitchen to see if he could help. It was all done and they set up a little table near the fireplace. It was perfect. They made a little toast and started to eat. She looked squarely at him with the slightest hint of a smile on an otherwise serious face. In a mischievous tone she said, "I saw your wife today."

"What?" He was mildly shocked and stopped eating.

"It was the oddest thing. I was grocery shopping this morning and I was on autopilot when my eye was arrested by this woman across the store. Not just because she looked so unusual, which she did, honestly, but because I recognized her from the pictures in your house." She had Robert's complete attention.

"I know she had no idea who I was, so I thought I'd just kind of wander over for a closer look. I'm sorry. I was curious."

Robert began to smile.

"Think about it," she said, "for all intents and purposes I was invisible to her. I could just walk up and check out the competition."

Robert winced.

"Just joking, but I did want to go up and see her."

Robert was thinking, right, probably two of the most beautiful women in the store wander toward each other and they would be unaware of each other. Beautiful women who work so hard on their appearance and then seem shocked when people notice. Even if they weren't completely aware of each other, he kept thinking, he was all set up for some kind of situation. Then she threw in the curve ball.

"Well, when I got pretty close to her, another woman walked up to her. I was completely in hearing range. She introduced herself, but I don't remember her name. It was obvious Maggie didn't know her. The woman told her that she recognized her from pictures or something. She felt she had to say something to Maggie about how grateful she was to you." Ressa stared at him.

Robert was about to ask her what she looked like when Ressa continued.

"She said you helped her son tremendously when they had been getting nowhere for a long time and that her whole family couldn't thank you enough."

Robert knew it was Patricia Nelson. How ironic.

"Maggie just stood there. Now I was beginning to feel like a voyeur. I had just wanted to see her up close and I had foolishly barged in on a very personal moment. Maggie didn't say much. She looked polite. I was a bit embarrassed and kept going. The woman left and Maggie stood there for a while before she continued shopping."

Robert looked at Ressa. He was speechless. She had no idea of the complexity of that little scene.

"The boy is a patient of mine. A special kid. The woman was his mother. That's some coincidence." He was still slightly stunned.

"I hope you don't think I was weird," she said, noticing the seriousness in his face.

"No, no, I would have done the same thing. It was curiosity."

The candlelight reflected off her apologetic blue eyes. Her dark hair framed her faultless skin, her lips were waiting to react. If he were a painter, he would paint the openness of that face. He was falling more and more in love with her.

The next morning, Robert met with Maggie as they had planned. Robert drove her to the airport. They seemed to be in agreement on all the details of the divorce and there didn't seem to be any hard feelings. They were a little early, so Robert stayed with her at the coffee shop in the airport until it was time for her to go through security. There was plenty of time to bring it up, but Maggie never said a word about her encounter with Patricia Nelson or the compliment. She had a lot on her mind, he thought. After they parted, he walked back to his truck, got in and just sat there. He wondered why she couldn't tell him about it. Were his successes just too small in her eyes? Robert didn't realize it, but he had reached Maggie as deeply as anyone could reach her. The strange thing was that it was Ressa who actually saw the moment. When Patricia Nelson walked away and Maggie went back to shopping, Maggie picked up a box from the grocery shelf and stopped, holding it in her hand. Her eyes floated, unconnected to anything in particular and gazed blankly right at Ressa. That was the moment. The moment when someone knows something before they are even aware that they know it, just before words are painted on a feeling that is already clear. That was the moment when Robert might have seen that Maggie loved him. But if you love someone and you never say it or you never show it, how can the other person know? What kind of love is that? Maggie was so well trained that she knew how to stop an emotion before it clouded her vision, before it threatened her whole creation. She couldn't tell Robert about the encounter because she wouldn't or couldn't put works on a lot of feelings, even for herself. Even if she felt it, Robert couldn't know it.

Chapter Seventeen

The Scandal

A couple weeks had passed since Maggie's visit. Robert and Ressa were spending a lot of time together, to the point where they were alternating staying over at each other's house depending on their schedules. This evening they were at Robert's house. It was a little after midnight when the phone rang. They both woke. Robert's thoughts went instantly to Sean. His heart sank a little. He hoped he was not having some kind of relapse. Had he gotten it all wrong? His mind was moving fast as he answered the phone. Ressa was not used to emergency calls in the night. She was alert and watching Robert's face.

"Hello."

"I'm sorry. I am calling so late." It was Maggie.

Robert dropped out of alarm mode. Ressa started to get up from the bed. She silently motioned for him that she would go downstairs to give him some privacy, but he reached over and held her arm, shaking his head emphatically, no. He gestured that he was the one who would go and he went downstairs to an office he had in the house.

"Hang on, Maggie. Just a second. Let me come alive." He gave himself some time to think clearly and get down the stairs.

"I was afraid you were asleep."

"It's ok. What's going on?" He was baffled. He could tell her voice was quick. After the last few months, this tone was unusual.

"I've been really stupid. I think I've been set up."

"What do you mean?"

"Six intern women in the department have come out with a harassment suit against several of the doctors. The District Attorney is all over this. He's going to make it a World Series debut for his career. The press is all over me. Richards must have known this was brewing, conveniently retiring before this all hit, getting me to step in to put a woman's face on the damage control. Daddy is apoplectic. He feels he was outplayed."

She was flying. Robert first wanted her to slow down. There was just too much information coming in too fast.

"Maggie, wait. Let's go a little slower. The first thing is that you weren't even there. How could you possibly be culpable? You are already sounding defensive. You can't do that for a minute."

"I'm having meetings with lawyers constantly."

"Of course, but do you have your own lawyer?"

"No."

"Well, I think you need one, someone good on the outside who knows the territory to overarch the tangle of all these players. Someone who will watch out for you, not necessarily the department or the university."

"Ok."

"I'm serious, Maggie. Right away. You know what I mean?"

"Yes, of course. So much has happened so fast and the press are obnoxious. I'm being bombarded."

"I think you should stay friends with the press. You don't know who or what you are up against. If they are coming to you, they think you're in charge. Perception is everything."

In the middle of his strategic thinking, he felt a funny feeling like someone was watching him, listening to him. Why do I react like Pavlov's dog whenever I hear her voice, especially if it seems like she's in need? She didn't even ask how I am. She only calls when she needs something from me. He couldn't really stop himself. Maybe he knew all too perfectly that it was this or no relationship at all and at least for now that's how it had to be.

"You've got nothing to hide. You can look like the savior if you're not defensive and you're confident that you'll get to the bottom of it and things will be better. When things get bad, most people just want a way out. They'll listen to you. They're not so tough anymore. Let the lawyers guide you, but remember they're going to be working for the school. What is the president of the university doing?"

"He's been quiet. Presidential. Let's get the facts, stay calm."

"Has he said anything to you?"

"No, the intonation is that he wants us to speak as one voice, wants intradepartment communication. Lawyers have the floor. They make the statements. The trustees are concerned."

"Of course they're concerned. If Augustine has a clue and there was some collusion, no one's going to talk to you and it's probably good if they don't. Maggie, you need a lawyer," he repeated. "Are you taking notes since it started? Good notes?"

Her silence meant no.

"Maggie, what if I call Bill Remington and tell him you might like to talk to him? Do you remember him? I treated his daughter."

Bill Remington was senior partner in a prestigious Philadelphia firm. He was a third generation lawyer and the firm was old school, very smart lawyers who were conservative team players. Their names would appear in the press only twice in their lives: when they were born and when they died. Every lawyer in that firm would laugh to hear it, but it was understood that there was no grandstanding. The firm was deeply connected to Washington, DC and New York and had a prominent reputation, especially in delicate matters. Like most powerhouses, they didn't like surprises and almost never were surprised themselves. They were so well researched they often knew the merits of their opponent's case better than the lawyers who were presenting it. They were so thorough and so good that if one of their opponent lawyers got sick, one of Bill's lawyers could easily run their case until they came back. Robert knew that at least if Bill couldn't help, he would know the right person who could.

"Maggie, it has to be someone on the outside. What do you think about Bill?"

"Yes. Call him and I'll talk to him."

Robert said he would call first thing in the morning, and then she could take over.

"These things take time. Don't trip yourself up. There's no hurry to answer anything unprepared. Don't take this the wrong way, but you may be on your own here. Augustine may be out of the loop. Besides, I'm sure he's about ready to have a heart attack."

"I know what you're saying."

"One more thing, maybe you weren't set up. Maybe they thought they had it figured out, but maybe it was fate. This could be a gift for your career to step in and put the fires out. You were made for this."

She wasn't exactly sure how to take that, but she thanked him.

"Can I call you?"

"Yes, of course. And I will call you as soon as I reach Bill. Please keep me posted and be careful."

When he hung up the phone his mind was racing, but he was not upset. In fact, it seemed normal in a strange way. Live by the sword, die by the sword, he thought to himself. Why would anyone want to live like that? He walked up the stairs. Ressa was up reading, but put aside her book when he came into the room.

"I'm sorry," he said. He gave her a rundown on the call. She told him he didn't have to explain. He assured her it wasn't confidential, it would be all over the news.

"Robert, I don't really need to know everything about your life. I understand your job and the necessary confidentiality. If you want to share something with me, then of course I would love that, but what I don't know doesn't intrigue me. It's more the not knowing everything about you that intrigues me."

She paused for a moment, thinking.

Robert, I remember my mother telling me how she really liked her father-in-law, my father's father. She said that if you had a conversation with him or even the smallest business dealing, he always respected that it was between you and him. No other siblings, no one. She said when she felt a little outside the family he made her feel special and equal. She always had this particular respect for him. She felt she could go to him with any problem, not be judged and have complete privacy. He automatically assumed his responses were equally privileged. It was just a given. That has always stuck with me. I don't think the confidentiality of a doctor patient relationship should be special. It should be the norm, not the privilege of some occupation or jurisdiction of law. It should be a common fundamental principle of respect, like my grandfather. I know there will be times when you can't tell me something and I respect that. The only thing I ask is when that happens, just kiss me. I will know everything I need to know from your kiss."

The room was dim. She couldn't see the tears in his eyes. He leaned over and kissed her softly, then laid back down on the bed. A kiss, he thought, how much of life has been revealed in a kiss? His mind jumped. He remembered something that he had forgotten for a long time. He had been a little boy about Sean's age when his father's father had died. They all went back to Scotland for the funeral. Robert could remember the narrow streets of the village perfectly. They walked on a narrow sidewalk between the lines of grey stone buildings that all seemed the same, cemented together on either side of the street. Only the rooftops seemed to vary, making the low skyline jagged. The only color on the whole street was the sign above the pub door in the middle of the town. It was painted black and red and white with black silhouettes of a hound and a cock rooster. They were all walking in the other direction, toward the end of the village where the mortuary was across from the great stone church. Robert and his mother and father stepped into the mortuary. The wake was over. This morning was the funeral. It was customary for the immediate family to have one last viewing of the deceased and witness the closing of the casket before the pall bearers would come and carry it across the street to the church for the service and later, the trip to the cemetery for the burial. A priest and undertaker were there in the parlor where Sean McPherson's father was laid out. Robert's father Sean and his two sisters were there with their husbands. Their mother had died years before. They greeted each other quietly. They had all been together yesterday and last night. They complained rotely about the morning's weather and just as automatically returned with, "it is Scotland, after all." The undertaker explained the procedure, that each of the children would have their chance to pay their final respects. Sean McPherson's youngest sister walked up first to the gilded golden kneeler that was placed at the middle of the coffin. She knelt down quietly onto the red velvet cushion of the kneeler. She bowed her head and said a prayer. Her husband stood behind her, off to one side. Soon her shoulders started quaking and the mood of the room turned more somber. She reached her hands into the coffin and grasped the white satin lining, gripping it with her fists, losing their color like a baby holding a blanket. She sobbed. No one rushed her, and in the right amount of time she quieted and stood up. Against her black clothing her white handkerchief fluttered like a little dove, dabbing and wiping, captured in her hand. It was time for Sean McPherson's second sister to go up. She was crying audibly before she ever reached the kneeler. Her husband behind her moved closer for support, but did not touch her. At the coffin she prayed. Then they could hear her talking to her father. She shook and cried for a long time and finally she reached into the coffin and placed her hand on top of her father's clasped hands, neatly molded by the undertaker on his stomach of his pressed suit. She rose, turned, and hugged her brother who was waiting behind her and her husband. It was finally his turn. Sean McPherson walked right up to the side of the coffin, ignoring the kneeler as if it were in his way. Robert followed right behind his father. Sean McPherson stood silently for a moment, then he leaned down and kissed his father. In his entire life, Robert had never seen his father kiss his grandfather. It shocked him. Even as a little boy, he knew the implications. Robert heard himself repeating to his father through a thickening throat, "Why did you wait so long? Papa, Papa. It's too late."

 Robert's mind drifted back into the bed with Ressa. The memory was still fresh. She had fallen asleep. He turned and kissed her lightly once more, careful not to wake her. He went downstairs and poured himself a whisky. He brought it back upstairs, turned off the small bedside lamp and laid down on his back with the glass in his hand. He took a sip. The liquid tinged his lips and a satisfying trace of heat moved down his throat to his stomach. He looked up into the darkness and took a deep breath. It was not too late, he thought to himself. It couldn't be.

EPILOGUE

The Hunt

Down on the flatter country, there was almost no snow on the ground. The bright sun reflected off the frozen ponds scattered like sequins across the dry brown landscape. In the distance, the mountains were white. By now all the ducks had migrated, but Robert knew of a place where he was pretty sure they could find sharp tailed grouse to hunt. At Sean's last appointment, they laughed about him showing up at the basketball game and Robert had asked him if he'd like to see the falcon and dog work. Sean told him he really would, so this was the day they had planned.

Robert had been flying the peregrine falcon a lot more. She was fit and keen. Since Maggie left, he had been bringing her in for a few hours in the evenings for company. Whenever Ressa came over, she loved looking at her. She was never an ill-tempered bird, but the result of all the added attention and interaction was she became even more social, friendly. She liked to be stroked lightly. Maybe it is the beak and talons, or maybe there is something more primordial about the forms of some animals, but a person doesn't look at or walk up to a falcon and want to pick them up and hold them close the way they can't resist with a little puppy. With a falcon, they are forced to ask permission to get close. How does a form control boundaries? Can anyone do it? Does it have to be learned through centuries of evolution, talons and beaks and thousands of years of stories? We respect the raptors. Maybe we even fear them. These things are so deep in our unconscious that we don't understand. Like a black hole, we know of its existence because of its effects on things that we can see and know. Somehow, everybody sleeps well with a dog at the foot of the bed. Almost no one sleeps well with a snake at the foot of the bed. What does a form tell you and what does it say about a person who is attracted to a certain form? She was a stunning form. A sleek animal with giant black eyes. The peregrine face is what grabs your attention first. They have black feathers around their whole head which continue into a black mask under their eyes so that they look like a fierce Maori warrior or menacing football player. All the black is offset by a trim of bright yellow near the nares, close to where they breathe at the top of the beak, which then turns back to black toward the powerful hook. If she opens up her long wings, the whole inside, like the lining of some expensive jacket, is a bold hypnotic pattern of white feathers striped with black that go all the way down her legs until the great yellow feet are exposed with the black, sharp talons. The pattern disappears near the top of her body so her neck is pure white, which only pronounces the blackness of her face. Her whole back is a sleek black gradient to a dark grey. There the black feathers are lightly tipped with white, almost the reverse of the front of her body. It is a majestic study of black and white and when she was inside the house she was even more arresting, she was so out of context. She and Griffin were becoming a great team. In the house, he would walk right under her perch. She was so used to him, she would barely look down at him only a few feet away from her. Griffin had been honing his own skills and was becoming a machine: strong, tireless, and obedient. Sam like to hunt with him. He thought Griffin would make a great dog to hunt with the rangier gyr falcons, which was a big compliment.

    Robert picked up Sean at his house. Griffin was excited to see the new face. He almost seemed perplexed by Sean's size. He hadn't been around many children, but he took to Sean immediately. Robert let him ride in the back seat of the truck. There was a console between the two front seats and Griffin rested his head on it for the entire trip, right next to Sean. Ordinarily, Robert would have made him sit back, but they seemed to be enjoying each other's company so much he didn't want to interfere.

They were heading north to one of the huge ranches where Robert had permission to hunt. By now, they were on a dirt road inside the ranch. They hadn't seen a person or a car for the last forty-five minutes and were coming up to the last leg of the trip, a fairly steep climb up an escarpment. The geography was spectacular. At the top of the rugged climb, the land leveled off into a huge plateau as flat as an airstrip for miles and miles. A rock altar, covered in green sage, lifted into the blue sky. It was ringed by snow covered mountains, but they were very far away. It was as safe as a place could be from eagles. When they got to the base of the escarpment, Robert put the truck into four wheel drive and began scrambling up the ascent. The truck rocked and stones shot out from under the tires. Sean was smiling and Robert drove a little faster than he needed to, having a little fun. When they finally broke over the crest onto the plateau, the scene was mesmerizing, like some living, breathing painting. The light and the atmosphere, the unmarred scenery. Rose colors, pinks, blues, and yellow pastels of the sky. Soft greys, greens and browns of the earth. The mountains off in the distance and not a single sign of human beings. It was as unspoiled a piece of land as anywhere in the country. Robert stopped the truck and turned off the engine. For a minute, the two said nothing, just taking in the scenery. Even now in winter, they could smell the intoxicating scent of sage all around. Finally, Robert looked at Sean as if to ask, what do you think? He didn't have to answer. Robert turned the truck back on and they drove a little further out onto the plain.

"Ok, it's time to get Griff out and let him start working."

Robert and Sean got out of the truck. Griffin was a little torn. He wanted to play with Sean, but his instincts were too strong. He began loosening up, making sweeps around the truck, his tail swishing, his nose searching, but he stayed close. Robert called him and showed Sean how to fit his collar with the telemetry so they could track him if he got too far away or hidden in some thick country. He showed

Sean the receiver inside the truck and which channels were which animal and what the signals could tell him.

"He moves big. We'll follow slowly in the truck until he starts slowing down, getting close to some birds."

Sean kept his eyes glued on Griffin. Even when he was out of sight, he seemed to know where the dog would reappear. Robert didn't bother him. He was clearly captivated. In time, the mood of Griffin's work changed. They both noticed it.

"Time to get out the falcon."

Sean smiled widely.

Robert stopped the truck and shut off the engine. Everything seemed so quiet. They both got out. Robert opened up the back and fitted the tiny antennae device to the bird's leg. Then he gave the glove to Sean.

"You can hold her."

Sean's face lit up. He was quiet, serious, but he wanted to do it. He didn't hesitate.

"When we get her out, wrap the leash around your fingers and your hand, like this. If she bates off your fist, hold the leash tightly. I'll help you get her back on the fist. When we get ready to let her go, we have to make sure we get her free of the leash. The last thing we want is for her to take off with the leash dangling where it could get caught on something."

Sean nodded a few times; yes, yes. Check, check.

Robert showed Sean where to place his hand to get the falcon to step backwards onto the glove. The telemetry was in place. The bird stepped onto his hand.

People don't ordinarily know how to move around animals. It's not usually their fault. Life has changed. They eat animals without ever having to hunt them or kill them. They can spend their entire lives in cities with almost no interaction with them. They have no experience. When they guess how to behave around animals, they are often wrong. Around a horse, they try to be respectful, they stand back, they are cautious. But they move too slowly. They make the horses nervous. It's like watching an innocuous scene in a horror movie when the background music changes and electrifies the audience. For a horse, the air is thick with suspicion. The mood is aroused and alert, defensive. It is not pleasant. The horses don't like it. Around dogs, some people know nothing of the dance of dominance, the social rituals of greetings, the vast amount of information that is exchanged. The person bends down, roughing up the dog's coat and starts talking baby talk. A person walks up to you on a city street. They start talking gibberish straight at your face. Even if you are not afraid, you feel uncomfortable. The rules of engagement are all going wrong, the encounter is confusing, neurotic. The dog doesn't like it. It takes a long time for a falcon to get used to the rhythms of the falconer. They are wild, and not very social. They can fly. They are fast. They have no need to suffer fools. If you are odd, they are gone. People think too much (or they don't think at all) about how they are being perceived when they are acting a certain way. They project, and depending on the size of their ego, they create a description of what is going on and then believe it. It is sad to see how estranged they are from their own family of the natural world around them. If such a person looks out of place in nature or acts out of place in nature or among animals, then Sean Nelson was simply the exact opposite. He knew how to handle the dog. When he got out of the truck, his voice dropped without tension. It was soothing and not suspicious. His sense of space was perfect. He knew where to stand, how close, how far. None of this was lost on Robert.

"From now on, we'll walk."

They both stepped clear of the truck.

"But first we have to take off her hood and let her settle and look around."

Taking off a falcon's hood is an acquired skill. Robert was starting to explain as he walked toward Sean in order to do it. Sean must have misunderstood Robert and thought he asked him to do it. Deftly, he loosened the braces of the hood and gently curled it off the falcon's head. Robert stopped still. It was eerie. It looked like Sam's hand. How could he know how to do that? The falcon shook its head. They almost always scan the country first, but she seemed to look straight at Sean. Robert had been the only one handling her, but she was totally at ease. There wasn't time to think too much, though.

"Let's head off toward Griff."

Sean walked off through the brush with the falcon on his arm. He never tripped on a stone or got tangled in the sage or slipped on some ice. Robert began to wonder why anything with this kid would be surprising. It was time to put the falcon up.

"Ok, Sean, just stand still. Thread the leash through the jesses on her legs. Let her just stand there. When she's ready, she'll push off your arm. Let her use you for a springboard. Stiffen your arm, but don't push her off. Let her go by herself, when she's ready."

Sean carefully slipped the leash off and waited. He stared at the beautiful bird so close to him. She ruffled her feathers once more and as they all returned and settled into place, she crouched and pushed off. Sean was thrilled, but he kept quiet. In a matter of minutes, she was arcing higher and higher in ever widening gyres. Now they all moved toward Griffin. Robert could swear that as the falcon drifted higher she was centered more on Sean than on him. He felt a little tinge of jealousy. Jesus Christ, he thought, it's my dog, my bird, and this kid is running the show perfectly. So much for self-importance. He was walking a little behind Sean when the scene began to radiate. It was odd. He'd had that experience in the summer, when the land would be so hot that the heat would wave and shimmer until he couldn't trust what his eyes were seeing. A flat black road would look like a river, a glittering lake would appear in the driest gulch, but this didn't happen in winter. Now the whole scene was in front of him. He was watching from far behind and could see himself and Sean walking toward the dog. He could see the falcon in the sky, but then he seemed to fade in and out of the scene. The vibrating waves seemed to make him disappear and reappear from the picture and he understood the message. It was not his dog. Sam could hunt Griffin in front of the gyrs; he could step out, he could go. It wasn't his dog – it was everyone's dog. It wasn't his hawk. She could hunt with this kid; they were working fine together. It wasn't someone's child, it was everyone's child. He could be gone. He was struck not by petty jealousy now, but by an overwhelming connection. There was no time to dwell on it; Griffin had stopped like a white marbled statue. Sean had stopped and was standing still, looking back toward Robert. The falcon was right over them, hovering almost at the limits of their vision. Robert snapped back. His vision cleared and his mind sharpened. He moved next to Sean.

"Can you see her?"

"Yes, yes. She's really high."

"Ok, try to watch her. We'll send Griffin in."

Robert yelled to Griffin. The dog moved in quickly and the grouse exploded off the ground. By now, the dog and falcon were a team. Griffin didn't just flush the birds, he tore under them. They would not be able to return to the ground quickly. He pushed them up higher into the air. The falcon was already in a blistering stoop. Lasered on the target, her wings folded back, streamlining into her tail, she was one perfect aerodynamic shape, her great talons tucked away in the space behind her torso like some plane's landing gear stowed away.

"Here she comes, Sean. Can you see her?"

"Yes!" He was so excited he could barely speak.

Robert was concentrating on the small, dark missile when she hit the grouse. It looked as if it was shot out of the sky with a shotgun. Feathers billowed everywhere. What had sounded like the report of a gun was actually the crack of the crash. The grouse spun down. It had died instantly.

"She got him!"

"Yes, she did."

Robert was trying to mark the spot where the bird might hit the ground. He was sure the falcon would circle sharply and dive on it again to make sure of the kill, but something strange happened, on what was becoming a strange day. She never stopped. She headed straight toward a second grouse that was still in the air. She had no pitch, no advantage from the speed of the fall. It was crazy. The grouse was too far away. There was no way for her to catch it, but she started pumping and she started to gain on the second grouse.

Robert and Sean stood there, silent at first. Robert couldn't believe it. What was she trying to do?

"She's going to try for the second one."

Now it was a horse race, with a great horse coming from way behind. Robert and Sean began to get excited. Forty yards to go and she was gaining on the grouse.

"Look at her, Sean!"

"Go, go!" he yelled.

They were both cheering.

Twenty yards. The falcon was still gaining ground and she had been up in the air now for over half an hour. In the last few feet, the grouse seemed to give up and the falcon bound onto it from above, riding it down to the earth. With a great spasm of her cable tendons, the eight samurai swords of her talons at once mercifully ended the chase.

Robert and Sean were awestruck.

"Seanie, you won't see that very often!" Robert practically yelled.

"Maybe she wanted to make sure there was one for you and one for me."

Robert grabbed Sean's shoulder, laughing.

"Maybe you're right."

They were both laughing that nervous joy laughter that comes when you have seen or heard or experienced something that was so good, so amazing, so rare and unreal that you don't know what the proper emotion is. Your rational mind has been tickled out of its staid composure, it giggles like an open-minded fool. It believes in magic. Something has broken the lock, at least for a moment. When Robert got to the falcon, she was not tearing out feathers as usual, preparing for a meal. She was still winded after the great effort. Robert was overwhelmed. He carefully made his way up to her and coaxed her off the grouse to his fist where he had a nice piece of quail to trade for. She hesitated only slightly and jumped to his fist. He let her rest a little and put the grouse in his game bag. He walked back toward Sean. He had calmed down a little.

"That was amazing. It doesn't go like that usually. I'm so glad you got to see it. I don't know if I've ever seen anything quite like that before. You must be quite a good luck charm."

"I couldn't believe it, she was so fast."

Robert gave Sean another glove and handed the bird back to him.

"Hold onto the quail and the leash tightly. She'll eat it all. I'll try to find the other bird with Griff."

Griffin had already found the other grouse and brought it back to Robert. They all made their way back to the truck. After she finished her meal, Robert put her back on her perch in the truck. He poured Griffin a bowl of fresh water. He had made a lunch so he and Sean sat down on some rocks, taking in the scenery. They replayed the hunt over and over.

If you want to tell if a person is truly right or left handed, it is not always useful just to throw them a ball. Too many influences may have interceded, training out the purity of the reflexes, clouding up the information. But if you kick them a ball, that pathway has not been so indoctrinated. Without thinking, they will kick the ball back with their dominant foot and you will have an answer. All day long, Robert had been kicking balls to Sean and every response had only made him wonder more. Who was this kid?

On the way home, they had to drive near the mountains. There was a road that followed a small river. The sheer faces of the mountains were close on one side, the tiny summer springs that dripped were now impressive ices cliffs standing hundreds of feet. They would grow until spring. On the other side were the wide-open, tan plains. The only reason the water of the river didn't freeze solid was that it was moving so fast, but everywhere the water misted or splashed or hit the air for too long, ice formed layer after layer into sculptures. With the refraction from the sunlight, it seemed like some mystical place, an endless ribbon of jewels. Low emerald green conifer branches hanging with silver diamonds, veins of blue topaz, opals and sapphires near the water, purple amethyst rocks on the edge.

Sean saw it first. He pointed up in the sky, further along the river. An eagle coursing. Robert told him to get out the binoculars in the glovebox and he would pull over. Sean got them out, but there wasn't any need for them. The eagle cruised closer and closer to the truck. They could see it perfectly with their own eyes. The massive dark brown form glided right over them. They could clearly see its great feet and beak. There is not a single nervous feather in the flight of an eagle. They lord over the skies. They both watched it pass at an even speed, heading off over the plains. Robert looked at Sean with a sense of ambivalent reverence.

"I have mixed feelings about eagles."

Sean looked him in the eye. "So do I."

Made in United States
Orlando, FL
13 December 2023